Brunettes STRIKE BACK

KIERAN SCOTT

G. P. PUTNAM'S SONS

Special thanks to Sarah Burnes, agent extraordinaire,
and to Jen Bonnell, the editor of my dreams.
For their unwavering love, support and encouragement I would also like
to thank my mom, my sister Erin, and my brother Ian.
Special thanks to Shira, Wendy, Ally, Manisha, Raina, Lisa, Ryan and
Liesa, all of whom believe in me way more than I deserve.
Your enthusiasm fuels the fire.
Most of all, eternal thanks to Matt, who keeps me going every day. You
are the ultimate cheerleader.

G. P. PUTNAM'S SONS

A division of Penguin Young Readers Group. Published by The Penguin Group.
Penguin Group (USA) Inc., 375 Hudson Street, New York, NY 10014, U.S.A.
Penguin Group (Canada), 90 Eglinton Avenue East, Suite 700, Toronto, Ontario, Canada M4P 2Y3
(a division of Pearson Penguin Canada Inc.).
Penguin Books Ltd, 80 Strand, London WC2R 0RL, England.
Penguin Ireland, 25 St. Stephen's Green, Dublin 2, Ireland (a division of Penguin Books Ltd.).
Penguin Group (Australia), 250 Camberwell Road, Camberwell, Victoria 3124, Australia
(a division of Pearson Australia Group Pty Ltd).
Penguin Books India Pvt Ltd, 11 Community Centre, Panchsheel Park, New Delhi - 110 017, India.
Penguin Group (NZ), Cnr Airborne and Rosedale Roads, Albany, Auckland 1310,
New Zealand (a division of Pearson New Zealand Ltd).
Penguin Books (South Africa) (Pty) Ltd, 24 Sturdee Avenue, Rosebank,
Johannesburg 2196, South Africa.
Penguin Books Ltd, Registered Offices: 80 Strand, London WC2R 0RL, England.

Design by Marikka Tamura. Text set in Garth Graphic.
Library of Congress Cataloging-in-Publication Data
Scott, Kieran, 1974– Brunettes strike back / Kieran Scott. p. cm. Summary: Still the only
non-blonde on her Florida cheerleading squad, sixteen-year-old Annisa makes some decisions
about how far she will go to fit in with her team while also staying true to herself.
[1. Cheerleading—Fiction. 2. Interpersonal relations—Fiction. 3. Teamwork (Sports)—Fiction.
4. High schools—Fiction. 5. Schools—Fiction. 6. Florida—Fiction.] I. Title.
PZ7.S42643Bru 2006 [Fic]—dc22 2005019908 ISBN 0-399-24493-X
1 3 5 7 9 10 8 6 4 2
First Impression

For some too-cool girls who always inspire:
Jaimee, Sarah, Anna, Ashley, Roxanna and Samantha.

"Go! Hey, here we go! Fighting! Crabs! Go!"

I thrust my fist toward the sky and grinned as the cheers of the crowd reverberated through my bones. I was never going to get used to the fact that the fans at Sand Dune High actually cheered along with the cheerleaders. I was never going to get used to the fact that they actually *showed up*. Back at my old school in Jersey, we were lucky if the entire marching band materialized. Even though games were mandatory, they were always finding excuses to skip out on watching our team throw interceptions, run toward the wrong goal and eat mud for four quarters.

"Go! Hey, here we go! Fighting! Crabs! Go!"

I glanced at my friend Mindy McMahon out of the corner of my eye and she smiled back. We were having one of those moments. One of those perfect moments when you just know that everything is coming together. The crowd was totally psyched. The squad was on. Even the weather felt like football. It was a cool night for South Florida—we had topped out at sixty degrees (I know, *shiver*), but because it was chilly by Sand Dune standards, we had finally been allowed to wear our little mock turtlenecks under our cheerleading vests. Honestly, we had been looking forward to this all season.

Meanwhile, on the football field behind us, the Sand

1

Dune High School Fighting Crabs were taking on the West Wind Dolphins in the county championship game. It was the rematch of the century! Well, okay, the decade. Okay, maybe the month. But still, it was huge. You could taste the tension in the air. Or was that just the overboiled hot dog smell coming from West Wind's snack bar?

We finished the cheer and turned to watch the action. Instinctively my eyes darted to the game clock. The last time we had played against the Dolphins, our archrivals, we had lost because of a mess-up by the officials involving the clock. Apparently they didn't know how to tell time. If anything went wrong tonight, this crowd was going to be grilling referee meat on the barbecue and serving it up for breakfast.

Okay, that was gross. But people were really pissed off. Still. Even though that travesty had occurred *weeks* ago. After all, the total injustice of what happened at that game spurred our football players and cheerleaders to go out and *vandalize* West Wind High as a finale to our weeklong prank war—an act that had landed all of us in jail.

Yes. Even me. Even though Mindy, Daniel Healy and I hadn't actually participated in any destruction, and we had been trying to sneak out of there, the Five-O nabbed us and tossed us in the big house.

Sorry. I hardly ever get to use words like that.

But suffice it to say we all wanted to beat West Wind now, fair and square. We all wanted it big-time.

"We have to get the ball back," Chandra Albohm, one of my teammates and friends, said in my ear, her voice as gravelly as ever. Her curly blonde hair danced around her face as a cool wind kicked up around us. "We have to get the ball back *now.*"

She was right. There was a minute left in the game. We were down by three points. The defense had to stop West Wind on the next play or it was over.

I looked down the track at the rest of the squad, lined up like sentries, their little blonde heads all in a row. I, Annisa Gobrowski, was the sole brunette on the Sand Dune High School varsity cheerleading squad. Well, the sole brunette who hadn't fallen victim to the peroxide fetish that abounds around here. Everyone stood with their feet apart, their hands behind their backs, holding their light blue and yellow poms. Everyone looked tense. Especially Tara Timothy, captain of the squad, our "fearless" (air-quote) leader.

Tara was the only cheerleader breaking formation, totally bizarre for a stickler like her, but it had been happening a lot lately. She clutched both poms in one hand behind her back and with her other hand reached up and rubbed the tatty blue ribbon that was wrapped around her long blonde ponytail. Her *lucky* hair ribbon, as she was constantly reminding us. I glanced down at her feet and grimaced. The elastic in her "lucky" socks was all stretched out and the formerly white cotton had taken on a gray tinge. This girl was falling apart.

The whistle blew out on the field. Time-out. I glanced at Chandra and Mindy. Right about now, Tara should be calling a cheer. Instead she was just rubbing her ribbon harder.

"Um, Tara?" Jaimee Mulholland prompted. Jaimee was one of the juniors on the squad and she was next to Tara in the formation.

"What?" Tara snapped, coming out of her trance.

"We should be doing a cheer, right? 'Cause it's a time-out?" Jaimee twirled her thick blonde ponytail nervously. "I mean, if *you* think we should."

3

Tara glanced around as if she was just now realizing where she was. "'Defense Get Tough'!" she shouted, turning toward the crowd. "Ready?"

"Okay!" we all shouted.

We executed the cheer, which ended with me and a couple of other girls up in double base extensions. I shook my poms as the crowd applauded, then dismounted into Mindy, Chandra and Autumn's arms.

"Okay, Miss Tara hasn't changed her socks *or* her hair ribbons since we won regionals," Chandra said under her breath.

"She's become a completely superstitious being," Autumn Ross said, brushing a lock of her white-blonde hair back behind her ear. "It's not healthy. Maybe we should stage an intervention. We could start her on a meditation program to help her de-stress. Oh! Or maybe she could use some acupuncture!"

"Come on, it's not that bad," Mindy said, though she bit her lip when she noticed the socks.

"I just hope she's not doing the same with her underwear," I joked.

"Ew! Annisa!" Mindy wailed. She shoved me with her poms, but she and the others cracked up anyway.

"Okay, if we win this game, then we're going to win at nationals," Tara said, loud enough for all of us to hear. Her two best friends, Whitney Barnard and Phoebe Cook, rolled their eyes behind her back. "No, we'll *place*. We win this game and we'll definitely *place* at nationals," she amended.

Sage Barnard, Whitney's little sister, twirled her finger in a circle at her temple. A couple of the other girls cracked up. I had never liked Sage, but right then she had a point. Tara was making up her *own* superstitions now. The girl was bongo-bonkers.

"Ladies!" Coach Holmes hissed from her spot under the bleachers. "Pay attention to the game, please!"

We instantly did as we were told. Coach brings out the cadet in all of us.

On the field West Wind called a play and Bobby Goow, Tara's boyfriend and the team's star defensive end, burst through the line and slammed the West Wind quarterback into the turf. Sack! It was exactly what we needed. I jumped up and down, screaming with the rest of the fans as Autumn threw her arms around me. West Wind would have to punt. We would get the ball back with fifty-one seconds to go!

My heart pounded as West Wind lined up to punt the ball. At this point, we pretty much lost the will to stay in formation. Mindy, Autumn, Chandra, Jaimee and I huddled together, clutching hands, holding our breath with the rest of the Sand Dune fans. The ball arched through the air, end over end, and came down right in the hands of . . .

Daniel Healy! My boyfriend! *My* boyfriend was going to have the chance to win the game!

Well, my maybe-boyfriend. We hadn't actually said the boyfriend/girlfriend words yet, but we would. Soon. I hoped. In my head he was already my boyfriend. But then, a lot of things go on inside my head.

Anyway, now Daniel was running down the field. He dodged. He weaved. A huge West Wind player came flying toward him and Daniel ducked out of the way and stayed on his feet. The defender sailed right over Daniel and crashed into the ground. It was a total highlight-reel moment. I could just hear the SportsCenter theme music playing in my ear.

"Oh my God! Go!" I shouted. "Go, Daniel! Run!"

There was nothing but open field in front of him. Suddenly he was zooming across the fifty . . . the forty . . . the thirty.

"Go! Go! Go!" we screamed, jumping up and down.

There was only one defender anywhere near him. The guy reached out to grab Daniel's jersey just as he crossed into the end zone, but Terrell Truluck appeared out of nowhere and took him out. Crack! A sweet block. And Daniel was in! Touchdown!

"Touchdown, number thirty-two, Daniel Healy!" The announcer called out as the entire team huddled and jumped and thrust their helmets into the air. Daniel and Terrell jumped up and smacked chests, celebrating. I hugged everybody in sight. We were up by three! We could really win this one!

Adam Rider kicked the extra point and now all we had to do was stop West Wind on the next play. They would have one shot for a Hail Mary. One shot to beat us.

Adam kicked the ball off. The entire squad was huddled together. Tara rubbed her ribbon like it was Aladdin's lamp. Some guy on West Wind caught the ball. If he could do what Daniel had just done, West Wind would win. But Bobby wasn't having any of it. He raced upfield and before the returner had taken a step, Bobby smacked into him head-on, drilling him into the ground.

Time ran out. And the world pretty much exploded.

"We won! We won!" Jaimee shouted in my ear.

The entire football team rushed the field. The Sand Dune stands emptied out in a wave of insanity. Everyone was hugging me and screaming and twirling around. The band was playing "Nah nah nah nah! Nah nah nah nah! Hey, hey, hey! Good-bye!" Which was exactly what the West Wind fans had chanted at us when they had beaten us last time. So there.

Flashbulbs popped. Someone was taking a ton of pictures and purple dots floated across my vision. All I could think was, *I have to find Daniel! He's the hero! My maybe-boyfriend is the hero of the county championship!*

I spun around in the crowd and there he was, looking right at me from midfield as his teammates slapped his back and celebrated around him. His hair was matted to his head with sweat and his face was smudged with dirt and grime. My heart stopped and then slammed into my rib cage in total elation. In that split second I imagined the movie moment in my mind. I would jump into his arms. He would lift me off my feet and twirl me around, my cheerleading pleats flying . . . .

"Daniel!"

Out of nowhere, Sage raced across the field and into Daniel's arms. Suddenly I was watching the movie reel exactly as I had imagined it, but I had been bumped from the starring role. Daniel laughed as he hugged Sage and swept her off her feet. Her blonde hair bounced like a shampoo ad as she clutched him in blatant adoration. Daniel wasn't hugging me. He was hugging his evil ex. My heart dried up like a tomato in the sun.

How could he hug her? They were broken up! And she had treated him like dirt, cheating on him with my very own brother in front of a house party full of people! And hello? He was *supposed* to be hugging me!

I had been crushing on Daniel since the moment I met him on my first day of school, and it had almost killed me when I found out he was dating Miss Britney-Clone, Sage Barnard. Okay, that may be overstating it, but still. I had pined from afar until she cheated and they broke up. I was all ready to be a shoulder to cry on for him, but then he admitted to me that he had been thinking about breaking up with her for a while. Eureka! And soon we were becoming maybe-boyfriend-and-girlfriend.

So I ask again, *why* was he hugging *her*?

"Annisa!"

Terrell Truluck—wide receiver, friend of Daniel's, thrower of sick blocks—stepped out of the crowd. He had a white streak of yard-line powder on the dark skin of his forearm and his shaved head was glistening.

"Whooooo! We did it!" he shouted, grabbing me up in a hug. I hugged him back, letting him swing me around, and forced a smile. With his movie-star smile and deep brown eyes, Terrell was pretty much a lock to win best-looking in his class, so if I couldn't hug Daniel, I supposed he wasn't a bad substitute.

"Great game!" I told him as he put me down again.

And then Daniel was there at my side. "Not as great as this playah!" Terrell shouted, slapping hands with Daniel. Daniel grinned and they did the manly, one-armed hug thing before Daniel finally, *finally* stepped up to me and enveloped me in his arms.

He smelled like a gym sock. His jersey was soaked through. Some mud rubbed off on my cheek. Still, I had never felt so relieved.

"You do realize you just won the game," I said to him. "You personally."

Daniel grinned sheepishly. "Nah. It was a team effort."

"Yeah, you just keep telling yourself that," I said. "That was an amazing run."

"Thanks," Daniel said as the celebration continued around us. "The guys are all going back to Crush's house for a party, but I was thinking . . . maybe we could go to Dolly's first? Just you and me? For some victory fries?"

My pulse raced so hard that my body temperature sky-rocketed. See? He's totally my boyfriend. He was probably hugging Sage only because she threw herself at him . . . right? One of these days that girl was going to have to start dealing with the fact that Daniel was *my* boyfriend now.

Maybe.

"I'm there," I said.

"Sweet," he replied.

He was just about to kiss me when a bunch of guys emerged from the crowd and lifted him up off his feet, hoisting him over their shoulders. I laughed at Daniel's stunned expression. The mob went wild when they saw the hero of the moment lifted up above their heads. A couple of reporters from the local cable station approached the insanity, gunning for Daniel.

"It could be a while!" Daniel shouted down to me as he was bumped away.

"I'll be here!" I shouted back.

And then I did what any self-respecting cheerleader would do. I leaped into the psychotic throng.

• • •

"Oy. You are just all kinds of barf-worthy right now," Bethany Goow said to me as we walked toward the West Wind High parking lot with the rest of the Sand Dune crowd.

"Gee, thanks," I replied with an eye roll. "And did you just say 'oy'? Are you Yiddish all of a sudden?"

"I can 'oy' if I want to 'oy,'" she grumbled.

Actually, Bethany Goow could say pretty much anything and get away with it. She of the black eyeliner, black nail polish and jewelry that could probably double as weaponry was my best friend at Sand Dune High. The antithesis of all my other friends who loved school and loved life, Bethany hated pretty much everything around her. Except me. And her website, sucks-to-be-us.com. She reserved a special place in her bile pit for her brother, Bobby Goow, his girlfriend, Tara Timothy, and all the cheerleaders, football players and pep-squad members at SDH. Again, except for me. She came to the games only to support me—and crack herself up by mocking everybody else.

I so wished I could introduce her to Jordan Trott, my bff from Jersey. The two of them practically shared the same brain from a thousand miles away. Unfortunately, I hadn't even talked to Jordan in days. We were both so busy lately, it seemed like all we had time for was prolonged phone tag. But I would *have* to get her on the phone tonight. Jordan lived for a juicy SDH update and she would know exactly what to say to make me feel better about the whole Daniel and Sage situation.

"Seriously, could you stop blushing for five seconds so I don't have to hurl on Sage Barnard's backpack," she said, glancing up ahead. She frowned thoughtfully. "Actually . . . that could be interesting—"

"Be my guest," I grumbled.

"Sweet," Bethany said, rubbing her hands together.

"No! I'm just kidding!" I cried, grabbing her arm. "I'm not

10

blushing anymore." While I wouldn't mind seeing Sage's face if someone barfed on her, I wasn't quite jerky enough to let it happen.

"Okay, so, I really want you to do an exposé on this whole nationals thing for the site," Bethany said, unwrapping a Tootsie Pop and shoving it in her mouth. "You could go around and ask all the cheerleaders which is their preferred eating disorder of the moment and—"

"Bethany!" I said with a groan. "I thought we were working on our stereotypes!"

Her dark eyes widened. "I am! I just—"

There went that flashbulb again, going off like a strobe light in my face. I squinted and instinctively raised my hands. Before I knew what was happening, I heard a scuffle, and when I was able to focus again, Bethany had a tall, skinny guy in a blue polo shirt pinned up against the chain-link fence that ran all around the football field. He looked vaguely familiar, but I couldn't place him. Maybe it was the look of terror in his eyes that was throwing me off.

"Bethany!" Jaimee gasped, jogging up from behind us.

"Somebody's been working out," the kid said.

Bethany ripped the camera out of his hand and let his neck go. "Ever hear of personal space?" she asked.

He looked and smirked. "Ever hear of small claims court? 'Cause if you break my camera, that's where we'll be."

"No need to sue," I said. "Bethany, give the nice boy his camera back."

Bethany narrowed her eyes and offered up the digital camera. The kid checked it over quickly, making sure nothing was broken. He looked at me and sort of half smiled, and suddenly I knew why I knew him. This was the guy. The guy

11

who had taken the most humiliating picture of my life. I *hated* this guy.

A few weeks back, during my very first pep rally at Sand Dune High, I had gotten overzealous and missed the foot placement on one of our pyramids. Thanks to my supreme klutziness, the whole stunt had gone down and this kid had snapped a picture of me with my skirt up and my briefs on display. As if that wasn't bad enough, he had slapped it on the front page of the school newspaper, the *Weekly Catch*, for all the world to see and save.

"Annisa, this is Steven Schwinn," Jaimee said with her ever-present bright smile. "Steven is one of my best friends. We've known each other since we were about five years old and he knocked on my door and asked my parents if he could swim in our pool. He already had his swimmies on and a mask and everything. And he was, like, breathing through a snorkel. I thought he was going to faint. It was so cute. So anyway, when he said he wanted to meet you, I told him I would introduce you, natch. You don't mind, do you?"

Did I mention that Jaimee is a natural babbler? And she asks permission for basically everything. I wonder if her parents are really strict.

"It's a pleasure, milady," Steven said. He lifted his camera and snapped a picture of my undoubtedly ill-looking face.

"Did you just call her 'milady'?" Bethany said, amused.

"You have a problem with chivalry?" Steven asked, arching an eyebrow.

"Yeah, it was very chivalrous when you took a picture of me with my skirt over my head and published it for the entire school to enjoy," I said flatly.

"That was one of my favorite shots of all time," Steven

said proudly. He looked into his viewfinder and adjusted some knob or other. "I have it blown-up on the bulletin board in the *Weekly Catch* office. You know, you should autograph it for us!"

Unbelievable. I looked at Bethany. "Him, you can barf on."

"Annisa!" Jaimee said, wide-eyed. She looked at Bethany like she thought Bethany was actually going to stick her finger down her throat.

Steven lifted his free hand. "I was just doing my job!"

"You have to take that picture down," I told him. "I'll beg if you want me to."

"*Real*-ly?" he said with a kind of suggestive grin.

"Okay, you don't know me well enough to look at me like that," I said.

"You're right. I'm sorry," Steven said. "Consider me shamed."

"I'd like to consider you invisible," Bethany said, rolling her eyes.

"I second that."

Bethany and I shook our heads and rejoined the crowd. I couldn't believe Jaimee was friends with this nutcase. But then again, Jaimee was one of those super-nice people who could be friends with anyone. You had to love that about her.

I noticed that Sage, Whitney, Tara, Bobby and Christopher had stopped up ahead to chat. I had no idea where Daniel had disappeared to, but my guess was he was being interviewed by those reporters who had corralled him after the game. My maybe-boyfriend the celebrity.

"You're going to have to get used to me, Annisa," Steven said, failing to take our not-so-subtle hints. He fell into step with me. "I'm going to be covering all of the squad's events

13

from now until nationals. You know, following you all on your road to glory."

"He's doing a retrospectacle," Jaimee said.

"I think you mean retrospective," Felice put in, walking up behind us.

"Yeah, right," Jaimee said, blushing slightly. "Anyway, he's even coming on the bus with us and everything. Coach Holmes said it was okay."

"Great. Maybe you can get a shot of me snoring with drool coming out of my mouth," I told him.

"Funny," he said. He whipped out a digital planner and powered it up. "So I want to schedule a time to meet with you one day this week. What's good for you? I'm free Tuesday."

"Why do you want to meet with me?" I asked.

"To interview you for my piece," he said, like it was obvious.

"Again, the question 'why me?' comes to mind."

"Yeah, why her?" Sage added, jumping into the conversation as we passed her by. I saw Bethany's fingers curl into fists. Sage's very voice sent Bethany's undies into a twist. Mine too, actually.

What was *really* irritating about her was that I had *thought* we were starting to become friends—or at least calling a truce. I mean, she had apologized to me for all the crappy stuff she had done to me in my first weeks on the squad. I had thought that meant something. But ever since regionals when Daniel had kissed me for luck instead of her, she had been back to her super-bitchy ways.

"Well, you're the new girl on the squad," Steven said,

14

addressing me and ignoring Sage. Nice. Maybe I *did* like this guy. "You're from New Jersey and I heard you never competed before. You're the perfect human-interest piece."

"Please! Her?" Sage said, pulling a disgusted face. "She's *so* unphotogenic!"

How this girl is in honors English with me, I have no idea.

"Sage!" Jaimee scolded.

"I'm not sure that's a word," Felice said.

"Whatever, I'm just trying to be honest!" Sage replied. "Really, Annisa, your hair is, like, ripped from *I Love the 90s*."

"You *sure* you don't want me to barf on her?" Bethany asked.

"Ew! What are you even doing here?" Sage said to Bethany. "Shouldn't you be under a rock somewhere?"

"And shouldn't you be off getting your lip waxed?" Bethany shot back.

Sage gasped, brought her hand to her lip and scurried off. Good riddance.

"Does she really need a lip wax?" I asked.

"Please! Haven't you ever seen her in natural light?" Bethany asked. "It's like Chewbacca molted up there."

"So, about the article," Steven said.

"Look, I got dibs on Annisa's story for my website," Bethany told him, looping her arm around my shoulders. "So you can just take your little camera and go interview the water boy or something."

"You can't have an exclusive on her!" Steven replied, his jaw dropping. "I work for the official SDH newspaper. We take priority over your underground web crap."

"Web crap? Oh, you are so dead!"

Omigod. The press was arguing over me.

"You guys!" I said, stopping in my tracks. "This isn't about me! It's about the squad!"

I was no different from anyone else on my team. Well, unless you counted the short brown hair and the occasional—*occasional*—pyramid-obliterating clumsiness. Besides, my relationship with most of my team was sketchy enough as it was. After all, I had made the squad only when two other members had been tossed over getting caught drinking—an event most of the team blamed me for, thinking that I had tattled on their fallen teammates. (Not true, but people believe what they want to believe.) The last thing I needed was for any of them to think I was trying to steal the spotlight or hog the glory.

"If anyone's doing a story on nationals, it should be about the team," I said firmly.

"That's just it. I'm doing a bunch of pieces, so I need a lot of different angles," Steven told me.

"That's why they call it a retrospective," Felice put in.

"Exactly," Steven said. "You'll just be one angle of many."

"Come on, Annisa, you should totally do it," Jaimee said. "I mean, if you want to," she added with a shrug. "You don't want to turn down your fifteen minutes, do you? I mean, unless you do."

"If you don't do an interview, I'm going to do the piece anyway," Steven said. "I'll just have to talk to your teammates instead. Sage Barnard seemed like she might have a lot to say . . . "

"You wouldn't," I said.

"Try me," he replied.

Bethany stuck her finger in her mouth and tilted her head toward him suggestively.

"Come on, Annisa! You should do it! Free press!" Felice said.

I sighed in resignation. "All right, fine. I'll do the interview," I said, my shoulders slumping as I started walking again.

"Freakin' mainstream press," Bethany grumbled under her breath.

I smirked and kicked at a soda cup in my path. Maybe Jaimee was right. Maybe it was time for my fifteen minutes. Well, at least my fifteen minutes with my skirt on properly.

"Annisa, I think you're going vain on me," Bethany said on Monday morning, picking a poppy seed from her teeth with her fingernail. No chance of her worrying about appearances.

I stared at my reflection in my locker mirror and blew out a sigh. I had experimented with a new gel that morning with disastrous results. My hair was all slicked to the side with a random curl at the end and a kind of shiny veneer. I had been going for supermodel slick, but instead looked like a forty-year-old soccer mom. The blue-collared shirt I had decided to wear did not help the situation. I wouldn't have been surprised if someone had mistaken me for the French II substitute.

"I just don't understand what it's *doing*," I said, pulling a brush through it for the ninety-fifth time. It sprang right back into place.

"Here! Solution!" Mindy piped in. She pulled her well-worn Miami Heat baseball cap out of her bag and handed it to me.

"But I hate the Heat," I told her. "I'm a Knicks fan. This would be, like, traitorous."

"You said *like*! Twenty-five cents!" Bethany trilled.

"You have been spending way too much time at my house," I told her. My dad charges me twenty-five cents for every superfluous *like* I utter. Lately Bethany had become his in-school representative. Of course, I had yet to pay her a dime.

"Fine. I'll let this one slide," she said, leaning back against the locker next to mine.

"Come on, Annisa. The Knicks have sucked for so long, I don't think anyone would blame you for a small amount of disloyalty," Mindy said with a grin.

"I'm going to pretend you didn't say that, to save our friendship," I told her.

It was so great that Mindy loved sports as much as I did. I wasn't used to being able to talk basketball smack with other girls.

"It's the hat or the helmet head," Bethany said with a yawn. "You decide."

I pulled the hat on and checked my reflection one more time. The gray cap was soft and broken-in and looked completely cute on me. As long as my brother, Gabe, and my dad never found out I had worn it, I would be okay.

I turned around and found Steven Schwinn's camera right in my face. He snapped a picture and grinned. His brown hair was slicked down, looking disturbingly similar to my own. Suddenly I was super grateful for Mindy's Heat hat.

"Could you warn me before you do that?" I asked with a grimace.

"I like spontaneous moments," Steven said.

"Too bad he hasn't spontaneously combusted," Bethany said. Mindy snorted a laugh, then slapped her hand over her mouth in embarrassment. Bethany smirked, but didn't pounce. Was it just me, or were those two getting along better lately?

"Okay, you need to erase that picture," I told Steven. "I can't have photographic evidence of me in this hat."

"Not gonna happen, my friend," Steven said. "That picture is officially my property."

What was it about this guy that made me want to smack him upside the head every time I saw him?

"Future paparazzi scum of America, everybody!" Bethany announced, clapping her hands. A few people gave her confused looks as they walked by. Steven grinned.

"Dude, that's not something you're supposed to be proud of," Bethany told him. He ignored her.

"So, Annisa, how's tomorrow after practice for our first one-on-one?" he asked, pulling out his little digital planner.

Yee-ha, I thought. *Alone time with Mr. Irritating.*

"You know, for a spontaneous guy, you sure are anal," I told him.

"Hey, I like organization," he said.

"Is there anything you *don't* like?" I asked, raising one eyebrow.

He started to answer, but his words were completely lost on me. At that moment, over his shoulder, I saw Daniel down the hall walking toward us . . . with Sage. She was wearing this cute little green dress and looked deeply tanned and pretty. Daniel was listening intently, his eyes trained on her face as Sage laughed and talked and threw about ten thousand flirtatious signals his way. As they passed by a window, the sun lit her blonde hair and surrounded her with this incongruous angelic glow. I had the sudden mental image of her sprouting wings and floating up to heaven with a harp in her hands. I kind of wished it would come true.

"When did those two start talking again?" Bethany asked with a mild sneer.

"Those two who?" Steven asked, looking around.

"Are you still here?" Bethany asked him.

"I don't know," I said.

I didn't much care whether Steven was there or not. Sage was touching Daniel's arm. Like it belonged to her. Like *he* belonged to her. Hello? If Daniel was belonging to anyone these days, it was to me. Not that I think people should *belong* to people at all. I'm just saying. "But, I mean, it's not like he can't talk to her just because we're, you know, together or whatever," I blabbered, throwing in a casual little laugh like I was just *so* enlightened. "He can talk to whoever he wants."

Stop touching him, you beyotch! the little devil on my shoulder raged.

"Wow. You are so evolved," Bethany said, in a tone that told me she knew *exactly* what I was really thinking.

"Well, I don't get it," Mindy said, toying with the string on her red hoodie. "Number one, it's rude to you, however evolved you are. And number two, how could he even talk to her after the way they broke up? I mean, she cheated on him in front of the whole school. I don't think I'd be able to be in the same room with someone who did that to me."

That meant a lot coming from someone who was part of the Sage Barnard Entourage. Actually, now that I thought about it, Mindy had been hanging out with me a lot more than Sage lately. Huh. Maybe I had officially won her over from the dark side.

Meanwhile, I couldn't tear my eyes off Daniel and Sage. They just *looked* right together. They paused by the water fountain so Sage could take a drink and Daniel just hovered there like she was the only person in the world. Hadn't he even noticed me standing here all slack-jawed?

Oh, how I wished I'd tracked Jordan down over the weekend. But every time I had tried her cell, it had gone straight to voice mail. And every time I had called her house, her little brother had cryptically told me she was "out." Why hadn't she called me back? I really needed her words of wisdom right about now.

Just then, Sage noticed me gaping and smirked. Looking me right in the eye, she plucked at Daniel's hair like she was picking out a piece of lint, then giggled at him and ran her fingers through it. I didn't even see how Daniel reacted. I was too busy looking at the floor and trying not to vomit all over my new Pumas.

"You all right?" Steven asked. At least he didn't snap a picture and capture my humiliation for all eternity.

My skin felt prickly and hot all over. I swallowed and nodded and attempted to smile, but it must not have been that convincing, because Bethany let out a little groan of frustration and hoofed it down the hall.

"Hey, Sage," she said loudly. "Did you notice that really funky smell in the girls' locker room after gym today?"

"What?" Sage asked, probably baffled by the fact that Bethany was speaking to her at all.

"Yeah, it was sort of like a rotting-eggs-meets-tampon smell and I swear it was coming from the vicinity of your locker," Bethany said matter-of-factly. "I just thought you might want to clean it out, you know, for sanitary purposes."

Omigod. She did not just say that.

Daniel paled and Sage looked like she was going to faint. "I . . ." She looked at Daniel. "I gotta go."

Sage scurried off down the hall and Bethany shrugged, then leaned down to take a drink from the fountain. I'll admit I was relieved to see the two of them separated, but the icky feeling in my stomach didn't feel like it was going away anytime soon.

What were Daniel and Sage talking about? For the first time in my life I think I was feeling kind of possessive. And I didn't like it one bit.

• • •

My body had never been so exhausted. I was sitting on the floor in Tara Timothy's family room with my back propped up against the couch. My legs throbbed underneath the coffee table. I really wanted to eat the slice of pizza that was on the red plastic plate in my lap, but I wasn't entirely sure I would be able to lift it to my mouth. My arms felt like a pair of potato sacks that someone had randomly attached to my torso.

"Hey, Annisa, could you pass me the red pepper?" Erin Bailey asked from the other end of the coffee table.

I looked at the little plastic bottle. "I really don't think so," I replied.

Whitney laughed, picked up the bottle and tossed it at Erin, who caught it effortlessly. Why did everyone else seem so totally fine when I felt like a side of beef?

"Feeling the burn?" Whitney asked through her chipmunk cheeks full of salad. She waggled her eyebrows at me and took a swig of her diet soda. With her short blonde hair and her model good looks, Whitney was often told she looked like Cameron Diaz. And you know how Cameron always wins that best-belch award at the Nickelodeon Kids' Choice thing? Well, Whitney was just as good at that too. I totally loved her.

Steven snapped her picture and she shooed him away with a wave of her hand and a loud burp, earning a few laughs and groans.

"Pardon my bodily functions!" Whitney said.

I watched Steven go and tried not to roll my eyes. He was certainly staying true to his promise to follow us everywhere. He had been there all through practice and now seemed to have a backstage pass at Tara's house as well.

"Think Tara's parents would mind if I took up residence in their family room?" I asked Whitney, leaning my head back against Jaimee's leg. She was sitting Indian-style on the couch behind me. "I don't think I'm ever going to move again."

"I know," Jaimee agreed. She patted the top of my head in sympathy. "I thought spontaneous toe-touches were enough. What was Tara thinking with the front-hurdlers? I mean, I'm all up for a challenge and everything, but my legs are totally jellified."

"I think you mean 'simultaneous,'" Felice corrected Jaimee, dropping down on the couch next to her. "Simultaneous toe-touches."

"Okay, walking dictionary," Chandra said, rolling her eyes.

"At least you guys can catch air," Mindy said, gingerly bending one knee. Her other, sprawled-out leg was about twice as long as mine. "Long legs suck."

"Wah, wah, wah," Chandra said, slugging on a bottle of water. She popped a Hershey's Kiss into her mouth and chewed. "You sound like all of those supermodels who swear they were picked on in high school for being scrawny and tall. I would kill for those legs."

"I would kill to be able to jump half as high as Tara wants me to," Mindy replied.

"At least she's keeping us in shape for basketball season," Erin said.

"No doubt," Whitney replied.

I sat up a little straighter. "That's right. When do you guys start that?" I asked. Erin, Mindy and Whitney were all on the SDH basketball team. They wouldn't be cheering with us for the winter season, which was going to be so bizarre.

"The team already started practicing together, but we got a bye for nationals," Whitney said. "We have to go the Monday after we get back."

"Ouch," Felice said.

"Tell me about it," Mindy put in.

I didn't even want to think about it. The squad was going to feel so empty without them. And we were going to have to have tryouts to fill their spots. New people on the squad? Disaster. I mean, they were still getting used to *me*.

"All right, everybody!" Tara announced, walking into the room holding a videotape over her head. "I know you were all whining while I was gone and I hope you got it out of your systems."

Mindy and I shared a smirk.

"I hold in my hand the videotape of last year's nationals competition," Tara said, pausing in front of the television, where a rerun of *TRL* was playing with the sound all but muted. "I want you to see last year's champions in action so you know what we're up against."

She shoved the tape into the VCR and stepped back. "Ladies, the Black Bears of Mecatur High School, Louisiana."

Very dramatic. You would think she was bringing in the U.S. Olympic gymnastics team or something.

We all sat back to watch the tape, but seconds into the

26

performance, we were sitting forward again. Jaws dropped. Chandra and Autumn exchanged more than one stunned look. Tara's eyes narrowed further and further, her head rotating along with the tumbling runs as if she had watched the tape five billion times. Which, let's face it, I'm sure she had. The Black Bears were unbelievable. Their tumbling looked like something out of, well, an Olympic gymnastics competition. They caught more air than a 747 on their tosses and their formation changes were quick and crisp. No one ever seemed out of step. When the music finally came to a screeching stop, we were all frozen in place.

Can you say "gulp"?

Finally, Chandra whistled, breaking the silence.

"Damn, those girls are tight," Whitney said.

"Now you know why I wanted front-hurdlers," Tara said, looking right at Jaimee.

Jaimee squirmed. What did Tara have, supersonic hearing?

"Oh, please," Whitney said, popping a cucumber slice into her mouth. "We can take them, no problem."

"Yeah!" Phoebe put in. "They're not all that. Did you see their expressions? Pathetic!"

"And the energy was totally not there," Sage put in. "You can tell they're all about the technical."

I cringed. Every time Sage spoke, I remembered her all over Daniel in the hallway. Did she want him back? Would he take her? Did she have any evil hypnotic powers that could entrance him into thinking he was still in love with her? I wouldn't put it past the girl.

"Yeah. We've got personality," Jaimee added. "Right?"

Everyone chorused their agreement. I pulled myself out of my SageandDaniel reverie to join them, trying to focus on

27

the problem at hand. Gradually we pumped ourselves out of our Black Bears–related shock. Still, I knew that the next few practices were going to be even more grueling than the last. If we were going to take on the Black Bears, we were going to have to do some major overhauling. Like, yesterday.

"I like the enthusiasm. Just remember this feeling tomorrow when we double our weight-room time," Tara said.

"I'm not even tryin' to hear that," Kimberly said, raising a hand.

There was a universal groan. I swear my muscles yelled at me: *Why couldn't you have been a* chess *champion?*

"Yeah, yeah," Tara said, grabbing the remote and turning off the TV. "Let's take it into the backyard and open the props box."

Everyone cheered and pushed themselves up from their seats. I put my hands up and Chandra yanked me off the floor. My thigh muscles were quaking, but I told them silently it was time to toughen up. We had a lot of work ahead of us.

• • •

We all gathered around in a circle on the patio in Tara's backyard. She placed the props box, a large cardboard box covered in yellow and light blue construction paper megaphones, in front of her and sat down on one of the lounge chairs. The props box was a little idea Autumn had brought to us after regionals. For the past few weeks it had been in the corner at every practice and squad function. Whenever we felt inspired, we were to write down either a compliment for a member of the squad or an idea to make the squad even better and put it in the box. Tonight we were going to rip open the box and read its contents as kind of a push to get us through this last week of practice before nationals.

There weren't enough chairs to go around, so I sat down on the cool stone of the patio in between Autumn and Mindy, biting my bottom lip to keep from getting too giddy. I couldn't wait to find out what everyone had written. Steven hovered around us, his flash popping every few seconds.

"Everybody ready?" Whitney asked.

"Rip into it!" Chandra called out, earning a raucous cheer.

Tara and Whitney unstuck the tape and yanked the top off the box, which Whitney tossed over her shoulder, nearly taking Steven out. He ducked out of the way at the last second and snapped a picture of the fallen box top. This kid did not miss a shot. Tara pulled out the first folded slip of paper and read.

"Our first prop is . . . 'I wish we all had lungs like Chandra's.'"

Everyone laughed and cheered. Chandra shrugged modestly as she unwrapped another Kiss. "That's what happens when you have four brothers. I need to be loud to survive."

"Here, pass this to Chandra," Whitney said, handing the slip to Felice, who passed it around the circle.

"Next up!" Tara said. "Ah, good one. 'Kimberly flies so high, I sometimes think she's not coming back down.'"

Kimberly blushed as we all cheered for her as well. The slip of paper was passed along so that she could keep it, and Tara dug in again. She read the prop silently and rolled her eyes, flushing. She handed it over to Whitney, who cracked up.

"'Props to Tara, our superstitious leader!'" Whitney read, throwing her arms around Tara to give her a squeeze. Tara

29

waved off our hoots and hollers and quickly fished out the next prop.

"This one's a suggestion," Tara said as everyone finally quieted down. "'We should all do community service together.'" She looked up at us. "Good idea. We should talk about that when we get back from nationals."

I grinned happily. That one was mine. Of course, if Tara had known that, she probably would have found some way to shoot it down. Anonymity was cool.

"'Annisa's constant pep makes me smile, even during math tests, when I'm usually in the depths of despair,'" Tara read, then smirked. "Wow. Poetic."

Everyone cheered for me and I was grinning uncontrollably now as Steven got in my face for a close-up. I had a feeling I knew who had written that one. I shot Autumn a look and she was blushing. Yep. That sounded like her.

"Another suggestion!" Whitney shouted, shushing the squad. "'Let's hire a gymnastics coach to workshop our tumbling.'"

"I bet those Black Bears have one," Erin muttered.

"No doubt," Kimberly said.

"Hey! I want only positivity here!" Tara proclaimed, putting an end to the grumbling. "But, yeah, they do have one."

Tara pulled out the next slip of paper, and when she read the contents, she went a little ashen. She clucked her tongue and read. "'I think Jaimee would make a great captain for next year.'"

Instant tension. Total silence. Jaimee cracked a smile wider than the Grand Canyon.

"Trying to get rid of me already?" Tara asked. She did not sound happy.

I glanced at Mindy as the rest of the squad shifted their positions and tried not to make eye contact. Jaimee pulled her knees up, hugged them and hid her grin behind them. Who was thinking about next year? It was only December. We hadn't even gotten through nationals yet. Next September seemed light-years away.

"Are we nominating captains? 'Cause nobody told me," Erin said.

Suddenly the entire squad erupted in excited chatter. Everyone was talking over everyone else, but all I could do was sit there. There was a pit forming in my stomach. Losing Mindy, Erin and Whitney for winter season was one thing. Next year was a whole other ball o'whatever. First of all, Tara would be history. As much as we had argued and clashed, I couldn't even imagine the squad without her. And it wasn't just her. Phoebe, Felice, Kimberly, Lindsey . . . *Whitney*. They would all be gone. Whitney was the first person on the squad who had ever bothered to be nice to me, and Phoebe and I had become friends . . . sort of. It was going to be so weird without them.

"Hey! Hey! Hey!" Whitney shouted, standing up. She stuck two fingers in her mouth and whistled. I have *always* wanted to know how to do that. Everyone instantly shut up. "We can't get distracted by this right now," Whitney said gravely. "We only have a few days until nationals. I say we don't talk about the captainship until after the competition."

A bunch of girls nodded their agreement.

"Good idea," Tara said. "So we're agreed?"

"Yeah!" everyone shouted.

"Okay. Let's get back to the props," Tara said. "I'd like a little focus here, people."

At that moment, my phone let out a loud double beep. The entire squad turned to look at me as I mentally willed myself to disappear. When it didn't work, I pulled my cell phone out of my pocket and checked the screen. There was an IM from Jordan.

Jordan: where ARE YOU!!!???

Instant guilt. Clearly Jordan had been trying to reach me to return my many messages.

"Goblonski? Hello?" Tara said.

Oops. Tara must have been really mad. She knew my last name now and mispronounced it only when her head was starting to spin. I turned off the phone and shoved it back in my pocket, feeling like the worst best friend in history. I would call Jordan the second I got home.

"Sorry," I said.

"Anyone put anything in there about not being rude during meetings and practices?" Sage asked.

A couple of people laughed and my face went from red to maroon. Did I mention how much I craved the ability to disappear?

Tara reached into the box and pulled out another note. Her face lit with a surprised smile. "'I think that, for nationals, Annisa should dye her hair blonde so we all look uniform.'"

Someone snorted a laugh. Everyone else went deadly

quiet. I'm pretty sure my brain went into emergency shutdown.

"It doesn't really say that," Whitney said, snatching the slip out of Tara's hand. "Wow. It really says that. Who wrote this?" she demanded, irritated.

"Whitney, the props box is supposed to remain anonymous," Tara said in a super-sweet voice. I imagined chocolate goo just dripping out of her mouth and glomming up her white T-shirt.

She reached into the box again and I blinked back a couple of hot tears. *Get a grip, Gobrowski,* I told myself. *It was probably just a joke. It was just one person's idea of a joke.* I glared at Sage from across the circle. If anyone would suggest I dye my hair, it would be her. She probably hoped it would come out orange so that I would be so hideous, Daniel would dump me and run back to her Jessica Simpson–looking self.

"'Annisa needs to go blonde!'" Tara read.

I blinked. *What?*

"Okay, you have to be making this up," I said, standing and walking over to them. I grabbed the slip of paper and sure enough, she had read it correctly. I didn't recognize the handwriting, but there it was, in purple ink.

"Hey! Here's another one!" Tara announced.

My blood was seriously starting to boil. "Are you guys serious?" I said, turning to the squad. No one would make eye contact with me. "You guys, come on! Uniformity? Other squads have all kinds of hair colors! Other squads have multiracial members! We don't all have to look exactly the same!"

More silence. More inability to actually look at me. "Aren't you going to *say* something?"

33

"Well, it's different with us," Maureen said finally, pulling at a tuft of grass that had broken up between the stones of the patio. "I mean, because you're the *only* one."

"Yeah," Lindsey said. "You gotta admit, the attention does go right to you. And that can't be good if they're judging the whole squad."

"You guys don't even realize how insane you sound, do you?" Whitney said, shaking her head. I felt a rush of warmth so strong, I just wanted to tackle her into a hug.

"Whitney, we don't want to tear anyone down," Tara said, trying to sound all Mother Teresa.

"Well, what do you think you're doing to me?" I blurted. "And Whitney's right! I mean, they're professional judges! You really think they're going to be stun-gunned by one brunette head? Okay . . . okay . . . " (I was in blind-rage-rant mode now.) "If uniformity is the problem, why don't we *all* dye our hair red or something? How would you guys feel about *that*?"

"Shyah. Like that's gonna happen," Sage said.

Would it be wrong to strangle her?

"Just . . . think about it," Tara said finally, reaching up to slap me on the back. "If you want, we can always dye it when we get to nationals."

I looked into her eyes. She was serious. She really thought I might do this. It seemed like she *expected* me to come around. I couldn't believe it. These people were supposed to be my teammates. My friends. And here they were, using this totally passive-aggressive method to tell me they wanted me to change my appearance for them. At least Whitney had stuck up for me, but that didn't erase the fact that Mindy and Autumn and Chandra and Jaimee hadn't. Didn't they realize how wrong this was? Suddenly I felt like more of an outsider than I had on my first day of school.

"Can I just point out that these don't exactly fall into the definition of 'props'?" I said.

"But they do fall under the 'ways to improve our squad' category," Tara replied.

Yeah. If your definition is looser than the elastic around your ankles, I thought.

I trudged back to my spot in the circle and dropped down, hugging my knees as close to me as possible so that I wouldn't touch the girls at my sides. I wanted a bubble of my very own. I had never felt so abandoned in my life.

• • •

As I dragged myself through the kitchen door at my house that night, I turned my cell phone back on. The second I did, it rang, singing the theme song from *The Phantom of the Opera*. Jordan! (Hey, she picked her own ring. Don't ask me.)

"Jordan! Can you please get in that crappy Jetta of yours and get your butt down here and save me already?" I said into the phone, dropping my bags next to the center island.

"Whoa. What's going on? More drama?" she said.

"You have no idea," I told her.

"Like Sand Dunes through the hourglass, so are the blondes of our lives," she said in a low, low voice.

I cracked up laughing. This was Jordan's current favorite line, and even though it made less than zero sense, it always made me smile. Actually, just the sound of Jordan's voice was enough to make me feel better. I still had a real friend out there. Someone who would never expect me to change. I sat down at the kitchen table and pulled the cookie jar toward me.

"What's wrong, Neece?" she asked. "Talk to Jordan."

I sighed hugely. "I would *love* to tell you, but right now I'm just not sure I have the energy."

"Well then, I have something that'll perk you right up," Jordan announced. "You, my friend, are in for a *huge* surprise!"

"Really? What?" I asked. Excitement sizzled through me, crowding out the sadness.

"Like I'm going to tell you! Then it wouldn't be a surprise!" Jordan trilled.

I pulled out a peanut butter cookie and chomped into it. "Well, then why are you telling me that you have a surprise for me?"

"Because I live to torture you, obviously," Jordan replied with glee. I could practically see her rubbing her hands together maniacally. Of course, then she wouldn't have been able to hold the phone. "But it's huge. Just *huge.*"

"Okay, now you hafta tell me," I said, spraying cookie crumbs everywhere. I rolled my eyes at myself, chewed and swallowed. "Come on! At least give me a clue! Wait! Are you moving here? Please tell me you're moving here!" I leaned forward, my feet bouncing up and down under the table.

"Not that huge," she said flatly. "But you'll find out soon enough!" She sang the word *enough*, dragging it out over three syllables.

"You suck, you know that?" I said, but I was grinning.

"I'm aware," she replied. "Catch ya later!"

Just like that, she was gone. And just like that, I was distracted from the squad and their insane grooming demands.

36

"Come on, Annisa! One more! You can do it! Push!"

I looked up at Whitney as sweat poured down my face. "Why do I feel like you're my Lamaze coach or something?"

"Okay. That was disturbing," Whitney said, slapping my shoulder. "Just push already!"

I held my breath and strained my leg muscles to push the weight on the leg press up and away from me. Every bit of my body was quivering from the effort, but I worked it. I bent my knees to bring it back in and my legs collapsed, letting the weight crash down with a huge clang. Everyone in the weight room turned to look at me.

"My bad," I said.

"All right, all right. Nothing's broken," Whitney said, waving them off. "Move it along. Nothing to see here."

I dropped my legs down on either side of the bench and let out a breath. This weight-training stuff was no joke. I dreaded every session in this room for a number of reasons. First of all, I always went home exhausted. Second, it smelled like hundreds of years' worth of sweaty armpits. And third? For some bizarre reason it had a bunch of windows facing the hallway so that anyone else who had stayed after school could walk by and gawk at us at any time. And they did.

Still, I had definitely seen an improvement in my stunts

and I was actually starting to get defined shoulder muscles. Soon I'd be able to give Angelina Jolie a run for her money.

"Here. Good job," Whitney said, tossing me a towel from my gym bag. I wiped my face down and sat up straight. As I took a gulp of water from my bottle, I watched Whitney readjust the headband in her short blonde hair. We were the only two people on the squad who couldn't make a ponytail.

"Can I ask you a question?" I said, swinging my feet around to one side of the bench.

"Shoot," Whitney said.

"What's up with the dyeing-my-hair thing?" I asked. "I mean, who do you think put those suggestions in there?"

Whitney rolled her eyes and sat down next to me. "I have no idea, but it's such a joke," she said. "No one really expects you to do it."

I felt a little better to hear her say this, but I wasn't so sure. "What about Tara?"

"Ignore Tara. You know how obsessive she is when it comes to competitions," Whitney said. "I mean, the girl's my best friend, but even I know that she's one strand short of a full pom right now. Just look at her."

Tara was practicing the routine in front of the full-length mirror . . . with her eyes closed. Honestly. Why practice in front of a mirror with your eyes closed? Every time she did a hand clasp, she looked like she was praying. And maybe she was a little bit. Winning was like Tara's religion.

Mindy replaced a couple of dumbbells on the shelf and walked over to join us. "I bet she put all those suggestions in the box herself," she said.

"Ya think?" I asked hopefully.

"Wouldn't put it past her," Whitney said. "Just do yourself a favor and don't take anything she says too seriously. Well, except the workout schedule," she added with a solid slap to my back. "That, you need."

"Gee, thanks," I told her, but smiled. I was glad Whitney was firmly on my side in the great hair debate. She was a good person to have on your side in anything.

Across the room, Sage and Lindsey chatted while they did crunches on the floor mat. My ears perked up when I heard Sage mention Daniel's name. I tried to tune in, but there was so much noise in the room, I could barely make out what they were saying. Had she really said his name? And if so, what were they talking about?

I was about to surreptitiously make my way closer so that I could eavesdrop when Steven crouched down next to them and took a couple of pictures. The second the flash went off, Sage squinted and sat up. "Ugh! Get away, perv!" she shouted, tossing her towel at him.

He stood up. "Hey, I'm just doing my—"

"Steven!" Coach Holmes called out, steering him toward the door. "You and I need to have a little talk about boundaries."

"If I see those pictures on the Internet, you're gonna get slapped with a lawsuit so fast, it'll blow your greasy hair back!" Sage shouted after them.

Just then Sage's pink cell let out a loud beep. She grabbed her phone from the edge of the floor mat and quickly scrolled through the message. Her healthy sweat-induced rosiness deepened and she let out a little giggle. From bitch to bubbly in 2.5 seconds.

"Hey, Sage!" Erin called out. "Who's the new man?"

"Don't bother," Whitney interjected. "She's keeping it all

a *big secret,*" she said with a hint of sarcasm. Classic sibling teasing.

Sage shot her sister a withering look and jogged out of the room, dialing as she went. My heart thumped with excitement. If Sage had a new honey, then maybe she *wasn't* trying to win Daniel back.

"You know anything about this guy?" Whitney asked Mindy.

"Only that he sends her, like, ten text messages every day at lunch," Mindy said. "She's keeping it on the DL."

"Well, she's clearly smitten," I said happily. "At least she's moving on from Daniel."

"God, it's so weird," Mindy said. "I can't even imagine her with anyone else."

My stomach dropped and Mindy looked at me, mortified. "I mean . . . you know what I mean . . . they were just together so long and . . . you know—"

"It's okay," I said, even though I felt like ralphing. Were Sage and Daniel one of those super-classic pairs that everyone was always going to see as a couple? Was it ever going to stop being SageandDaniel and become AnnisaandDaniel? They had been together since middle school, and since I wasn't even sure if Daniel *wanted* to be my boyfriend, it was kind of like he still belonged to her in a way. I'll admit it. I was straight-up jealous. Of *Sage.*

Ugh.

"I'm sorry," Mindy replied, biting her lip.

"It's fine. Really," I said as calmly as possible. And I meant it . . . sort of. I wasn't mad at her, just a little irritated at the situation. Why couldn't I have fallen for someone who didn't have a super-popular, totally gorgeous, ever-present ex-girlfriend? I shot Mindy a smile, stood up and grabbed my MP3 player out of my gym bag. "I think I'm gonna go use the punching bag for a little while."

I popped my earphones in and cranked up the volume. A little expending of nervous energy was exactly what the doctor ordered at that moment. I swear I saw the punching bag flinch as I approached.

• • •

Steven Schwinn was waiting for me outside the locker room an hour later, looking eager. He had disappeared for a while after Coach had intervened, but it looked like he was back in action.

"Am I going to have to get a restraining order?" I asked him, hoisting my gym bag onto my shoulder with much effort. Between gym clothes, practice clothes and my book bag full of homework, I was going to become a hunchback.

"Here, let me get that," Steven offered. I was about to protest, but he had already slipped the bag off my arm and my muscles were so relieved, I would have been an idiot to say no.

"Thanks."

For a guy who claimed to be all about chivalry, this was the first gentlemanly thing I had seen him do yet. Maybe he was redeemable. Or maybe he was just being nice so I would give him a good interview. I'd have to wait and see.

"No prob," he replied. "So I was thinking I'd walk you home and we could start the interview on the way."

I blinked. "How did you know I live within walking distance?"

"I do my research," he said with a wide smile. He had the straightest teeth I had ever seen. He pulled a tape recorder out of his pocket and hit RECORD. "You game?"

I shrugged. "I guess."

We headed out the back door together and cut across the football gridiron. I lived a few houses down from the back entrance to the athletic fields and took this shortcut every day. Daniel and I usually walked home together, but after the county championship game, his season was officially over and jazz band—which he had decided to do over wrestling, though he hadn't talked to his dad about it yet—hadn't started. He had been home for a couple of hours, probably kicking back with some corn chips while I lifted weights and struggled through push-ups. Oh, to be a football player instead of a cheerleader.

The sun was already setting and clouds were gathering overhead. A stiff wind blew my sweaty hair back from my face and I drew my sweatshirt closer to me.

"So, what are the differences between living here and living in New Jersey?" Steven asked, holding up the tape recorder. My bag bumped against his left hip while his messenger bag full of books bumped against his right. He looked kind of like a Sherpa.

"Are you okay with all that stuff?" I asked. After all, he wasn't exactly a bodybuilder type—more of a string bean.

"I'm fine," he replied. "And I get to ask the questions."

I raised my hands in surrender. "Okay, okay. The difference between here and New Jersey. Well, for one, there's about eight inches of snow on the ground up there right now, according to my friend Jordan."

"Jordan? Old boyfriend?" he asked.

"Uh . . . no. Jordan's a girl," I said.

"Oh . . . cool. Was she on the cheerleading squad with you?"

"Yep. She's still on it," I replied with a nod.

"Are they into competing too?"

I had to laugh at that one. "That would be a no," I said. "Honestly, they're pretty much the exact opposite of the Sand Dune squad. I mean, if my new squad met my old squad, the universe might collapse in on itself."

"I don't think that's scientifically possible," Steven said with a smirk.

"Trust me, you'd see it happen," I told him, trying to visualize what the meeting might be like. "Omigod, I can just see Tara Timothy and Gia Kistrakis in the same room together. They would kill each other."

"Gia Kistrakis?" Steven asked.

I glanced at him and suddenly recalled I was being taped. "Oh, God. Could you not print any of that?" I said, blanching. I tried to mentally replay everything I had just said, but came up blank. Still, it didn't feel like anything I wanted to have printed.

"You consented to an interview," Steven said.

"Come on!" I replied. "I'm known for my verbal diarrhea. I could say something that would get me blackballed forever!"

Steven grinned. "Sweet!"

All I was doing was exciting him. Mental note: reporters = untrustworthy.

"Look, if you don't give me the right to strike anything I say, then this interview is over," I said, pausing as we stepped onto the sidewalk.

43

"Please! I wouldn't give that to anyone!" Steven protested.

"Okay, then give me my bag," I replied, holding out my hand.

Steven stared at me, trying to figure out if I was serious. "All right, fine," he said finally. "But you owe me."

I grinned. "Cool." Score one for me.

We started walking again. "So . . . Gia Kistrakis?"

"Okay, Gia Kistrakis was this girl on my old squad in Jersey. She was like every stereotype you have in your head of Jersey girls, all wrapped into one," I explained. "Imagine Adriana from *The Sopranos*, but scarier."

Steven whistled.

"Tell me about it," I said. "This one time, the other school's mascot—a tiger—came loping across the basketball court at halftime to try to have some fun with us. It's like one of those big, orange, furry things, you know? So she's bending down to tie her laces and he pokes her on the shoulder. Without even, like, a *second* of hesitation, Gia turns around and just flat-out decks him."

"You're kidding!" Steven said.

"I swear! She thought he was some guy trying to look up her skirt or something. Anyway, she hit him so hard, his head spun around. Then he goes stumbling backward, totally blind, and takes out the scorer's table." I was cracking up hard now and Steven started to laugh too. "All these papers go flying and that little ancient box thing that controls the scoreboard cracks against the wall—sparks everywhere—and the tiger's uniform catches fire. Now he's running around, blind and on fire, and it takes, like, five of the basketball players to tackle him with towels to put him out."

"You're making this up," Steven said, laughing.

I paused at the end of my driveway, doubling over. I don't know if it was the story, the nostalgia or the sheer exhaustion, but I couldn't stop laughing. I was laughing so hard, I was wailing.

"Oh my God. Oh my God," I repeated, tears coming to my eyes. I gripped his arm for support. "It was *classic*."

"Annisa?"

I stood up and caught my breath. Daniel was pushing himself up from my front step. My heart went all spastic on me the second I saw him standing there looking all perfect. My heart pretty much always does that when Daniel's around.

"Hey!" I said, pleasantly surprised. My hand went directly to my hair, which probably looked like a bad toupee at this point.

Daniel glanced at Steven and stood up. He had his backpack and a copy of *Hamlet* in his hands. "Hey," he said to me. "What's up, man?" he said to Steven.

"Hi." Steven hit the stop button on the tape recorder.

"What's up?" I asked.

"I was thinking maybe we could hang out for a while," Daniel said, lifting the book. "Do some homework?"

Daniel was acting weird. Like he had been caught doing something wrong. His eyes were darting around and he shifted his weight from foot to foot.

There was nothing I wanted more than to say yes. Then we could go inside, spend a little quality time with Shakespeare—and each other—and I could find out why he was looking so . . . nervous. But I couldn't. Why did he have

45

to pick tonight of all nights to surprise me at my house, wearing that light blue sweatshirt that made his eyes look just like the ocean on a perfect sunny day?

"Actually, I kind of promised Steven an interview," I said, biting my lip. "We just got started."

Daniel glanced at Steven. "Oh, right. Okay," he said.

"Are you all right?" I asked him.

"Sure. Fine," Daniel said. "You?"

For some reason, the way he said *you* almost sounded like an accusation. What was going on here? Before I could answer, Steven switched the tape recorder back on and held it up.

"So, I'm here with Annisa Gobrowski and Daniel Healy, hero of last week's county championship game against the West Wind Dolphins," Steven said in a *Fox News Live* kind of voice. "I have to ask, are you two a couple?"

Time stood still. A rumble of thunder off in the distance punctuated his question. I saw a bolt of lightning flash, hit me in the head and turn me to charbroiled dust. Not really, but I was kind of hoping for it.

I looked at Daniel. Daniel looked at me. *Well?* I thought. *Are we a couple, Daniel?*

"What kind of interview is this, exactly?" Daniel asked. He looked kind of green now.

"The public wants to know," Steven replied. "Are you guys boyfriend and girlfriend or what?"

I swallowed hard.

Daniel looked me right in the eyes. "I think I'll just call you later," he said, sort of loudly. Then he rushed out of there so fast, his track coach would have been proud.

"Wow. Talk about dodging a question," Steven said.

He had no idea how much that comment stung. The first raindrop smacked against my forehead and I headed for the front door.

"You coming?" I asked him, feeling numb.

He grinned and slipped by me into the house. I stared at the edge of the driveway, wishing Daniel would miraculously reappear. He had just ditched the perfect opportunity to tell the world that we were a couple. I was really starting to wonder—did Daniel Healy even *want* to be my boyfriend? Did he want to be with me at all?

"So, Annisa, what's your favorite color?" Steven asked, holding the microphone to my face.

"Red, why?" I asked, confused. I think I was having an out-of-body experience.

"Favorite candy?" he asked.

I walked into the living room and lowered my extremely heavy body onto the couch. That was when I noticed that the entire place smelled like my dad's roasted chicken.

"Annisa? Is that you?" my father called as he walked in from the kitchen. "Oh, hello," he said when he saw Steven standing there.

Dad's brown hair was mussed, as always, and he had one pair of glasses on top of his head and another on his nose. Classic. Plus he was wearing a brown cotton sweater over black corduroy pants. We had lived in Florida for over two months and he had yet to grasp the fact that he should stop dressing for winter weather. Instead, he just kept the AC pumped up to simulate New Jersey winter so that we all had to walk around in wool sweaters and sweat socks. Dad's a highly sought-after college English professor and sometimes I think he's the definition of the absentminded prof.

"You must be Mr. Gobrowski," Steven said, reaching out his free hand to shake with my dad. "I'm Steven Schwinn, reporter for the *Weekly Catch*."

"Pleased to meet you, Steven," my father said, wiping his hands on the kitchen towel he was toting before shaking with him.

"Do you know what Annisa's favorite candy is?" Steven asked.

"Gummy bears and peanut M&M's," my father said automatically. "Why do you ask?"

"I'm doing a piece on her for the paper," Steven explained.

"Really? On Annisa?" my dad asked, looking impressed. He came around the couch and dropped down next to me. Steven removed both our bags from his person and took the chair on the other side of the coffee table.

"It's really not that big a deal," I said flatly. *What is a big deal is Daniel and the way he ran out of here. DanielDanielDaniel.*

"How about her favorite band?" Steven asked.

"The Beatles," my father said with a proud smile. "My daughter loves the classics."

As Steven continued to grill my dad on the most bizarre list of questions, I just sat there, watching as fat raindrops pounded against the living room window. I had a few questions myself. Like, why had Daniel bolted? And was he really going to call me later? Because it didn't feel like it. Damn. I was really having a hard time keeping up my normal glass-is-half-full outlook lately. Was this what love did to you?

• • •

"So," Daniel said, running his hands up and down the steering wheel of his black Honda Civic.

"So," I replied.

Yeah. This is fun.

It was Wednesday night and Daniel and I were sitting at the end of Chandra's jam-packed driveway. Tomorrow morning the squad was leaving for nationals and we had decided to have a pre-competition sleepover, just like we had before regionals. Partially because it had been so much fun the last time and partially because Tara was insisting we do everything in the exact same way so as not to jinx ourselves.

One of these days that girl was really going to need to get her head examined.

Of course, one thing had been different the night before regionals—for me at least. Back then I had known for sure that Daniel liked me. Now, even though he was less than a foot away, it felt like there was a monster ditch between us. One I couldn't seem to jump over. We had barely spoken in the last twenty-four hours and I had almost been surprised when he had actually shown up at our prearranged time to drive me over here.

I looked at Daniel's profile and my pulse roared in my ears. There was *one* way to jump the chasm. If I was brave enough. All I had to do was ask him. Just flat-out ask him. Then at least I would know. And knowing, one way or another, would be a lot better than this not knowing . . . right? Daniel looked at me and I instantly glanced away.

Oh yeah, I'm brave. Sign me up for *Fear Factor*, people, 'cause fear is not a factor for me.

"Is everything okay?" Daniel asked.

I pressed my sweaty palms into my jeans. "Uh . . . yeah. Just a little nervous about nationals."

Liar. Big, fat, honking liar. My nose grew so fast, it shattered the windshield.

"Well, maybe you should do something to get your mind off of it," Daniel said. "You know, distract yourself."

"Like what?" I asked.

He pulled me toward him and before I could even gasp in surprise, he pressed his lips to mine. My heart completely soared as I slipped my arms around his neck. Daniel pulled me as close to him as possible with the manual shift between us. It was the longest, deepest kiss we had ever shared. I could barely even catch my breath. Well, that was one way to bridge the proverbial gap.

He likes me! He really likes me!

Finally he broke away, but he touched his forehead to mine. Our noses were rubbing and his breath was quick and warm against my face. My lips hummed pleasantly.

Sigh.

Just ask him! my mind wailed as it swam and swirled. *Just do it!*

"Hey," I said.

"Yeah?" he replied.

"Remember that whole thing with Steven yesterday?"

Daniel sat up straight, and with his warmth removed, I felt like shivering. "Yeah," he said, his brow wrinkling.

"Well, he wanted to know something, remember?" I said, stalling. "The question he asked? When he turned his tape recorder back on . . . ?"

Daniel looked at me, his eyes blank. I had absolutely no clue what he was thinking. I wanted to scream in total frustration. He was really going to make me say it.

"Are you my boyfriend or what?" I blurted.

Oh, yeah. Way smooth, I chided myself. *Why you've never had a boyfriend, Annisa, I do not understand.*

Daniel blinked. "Your boyfriend?" His voice squeaked. He couldn't have looked more terrified if I'd just tossed him out of an airplane without a chute.

"I'm just kidding," I heard myself say as panic set in, jangling every organ in my body. I scrambled for the door handle. I had to get out of there. "I mean, you don't have to answer that, I was just . . . you know . . . wondering. Not that it's *important,* in fact, it's not important. To me, I mean." He was completely ashen at this point. "I don't even *want* a boyfriend, you know? It's, like, so yesterday, the whole boyfriend-girlfriend thing, right? I mean, hello? What am I, living in 1950? Just fit me for a poodle skirt and a beehive."

Did you just say "beehive"? Abort! Abort now!

"I gotta go. Thanks for the ride!"

And then I practically fell out of the car. By the time I got inside Chandra's house, I felt like crumbling to the tile floor. Would a permanent voice box removal hinder my future as a cheerleader?

"Chandra? Where are the M&M's for the oatmeal–peanut butter–M&M cookies?" Tara asked, one hand on her hip. Just like before regionals, she was wearing her Badtz Maru night-shirt, and Badtz was so washed out, it was clear she'd been wearing him every night since as well. Now I *really* started to wonder about her underwear.

"They were out of regular M&M's, so I got chocolate chips instead," Chandra said as she stirred the gloopy dough with a big wooden spoon.

Everyone else in Chandra's huge, professionally equipped kitchen froze. I stopped cramming our empty Chinese food containers into the big green garbage bag. Sage nearly dropped the pitcher of virgin strawberry daiquiris. Jaimee paused with a handful of avocado face mask just inches from Mindy's skin. Even Felice looked up from her copy of *The Canterbury Tales*, and it's next to impossible to distract that girl when she's reading.

"Are you sure you didn't just *eat* all the regular M&M's?" Tara snapped.

"Tara!" Whitney scolded.

"What? We all know she's a total chocoholic! I mean, I really can't believe they were *out* of regular M&M's," Tara said, her voice high and tight. "What kind of supermarket runs out of regular M&M's?"

Chandra finally realized the gravity of her faux pas. She stopped stirring and took a step away from our captain. "Okay, Tara. Stay calm."

"You couldn't go to another store and *find* regular M&M's?" Tara asked, gripping the edge of the counter. "Last time we did this we had oatmeal–peanut butter–*M&M* cookies, Chandra. Not oatmeal–peanut butter–*chocolate chip* cookies."

For the first time ever, Chandra was at a loss for words. That incongruity was almost as disturbing as Tara's dilated pupils. Chandra shot Whitney a helpless look over Tara's coiled shoulders. *"Help?"* she mouthed.

"Okay! I'm going!" Whitney announced, grabbing her keys and purse. "I'm going to get some M&M's. Let's everyone chill! Crisis averted."

"I'll go with you," Phoebe offered, jumping off the stool by the breakfast bar. I could tell she just wanted to escape the insanity. Together they hustled for the door, Whitney in her gray sweats, Phoebe in her pink-and-white-striped flannel pj pants.

"Just hurry back!" Tara called after them.

The front door slammed and everyone returned to what they were doing, though no one ventured within a three-foot radius of Tara. If and when she exploded, I knew I didn't want to be anywhere near her either.

"I'm going to the living room to make sure all our sleeping bags are arranged properly," Tara announced. "By the time I get back, there had better be some J. Lo on that CD player," she said, pointing at the flat, state-of-the-art, wall-mounted stereo. "We need to listen to J. Lo, just like last time, no matter how cringe-worthy it is."

"You got it, *mein Führer*," Chandra said under her breath, jabbing at the cookie dough.

"Her aura is so splotchy," Autumn put in, her eyes wide. "Do you think she'll let me cleanse it?"

"The girl doesn't even wash her socks," I replied. "I think her aura is out of the question."

I tied off the garbage bag and hoisted it over my shoulder, heading out the back door to the garage where Chandra's family kept the garbage cans.

"How nice!" Sage said with a snort, topping off Erin's daiquiri. "We finally found the perfect job for Annisa."

I paused, stunned. *What did I ever do to you?* I thought. What I said was, "There's still room in here for you if you want to climb on in. I'm sure you'll feel right at home."

"Ooooh," a couple of girls said. I couldn't believe it. A comeback! Right when I actually needed one! Who knew it was possible?

Sage put down the pitcher, picked up her cell phone and stepped up to me, glaring into my eyes. "At least *I'm* not Daniel Healy's sloppy seconds."

Holy crapola. She did not actually just say that to me! I ripped open the garbage bag and dumped the entire smelly, saucy contents all over her and her pink nightgown.

Well, not really. But in my imagination, it was *perfection*.

"Sage!" Mindy gasped.

At that moment, Sage's cell phone trilled. She checked the caller ID and raced from the room, her ponytail bouncing. Everyone looked at me.

My heart sank like a stone. Now I knew exactly what

Sage thought of me—as did everyone else on the team. She thought I wasn't worthy of Daniel. Did that mean she wanted him back? And if so, what was she doing with this new crush she was so excited about? Just stringing him along? She *had* made out with my brother, Gabe, while she was still with Daniel. Apparently Sage was a two-guy type of girl. Meanwhile, I couldn't even get the one guy I liked to officially ask me out.

I sighed and headed out back. Just then, I felt like Sage was completely right—trash duty *was* the perfect job for me.

• • •

That night, I was just crawling into my cushy sleeping bag, my stomach full of oatmeal–peanut butter–M&M cookies, ready to put the day behind me and start fresh, when Tara returned from the bathroom and clapped her hands together.

"So! Are we dyeing Annisa's hair tonight or what?" she asked, all pep.

My over-full stomach flipped dangerously. Everyone looked at me.

"Tara—" Whitney began.

"What? I'm sure Chandra has an extra box of dye around here somewhere," Tara said with a shrug.

"Hey!" Chandra protested.

"Don't even try it, girl. You're looking a little ratty around the roots there," Kimberly said.

"You want to talk hair issues, split-end?" Chandra shot back.

"Here we go," Erin said under her breath. She pulled her pillow over her face and held it there. A no-skirt-wearing (except for her uniform) tomboy, Erin probably had less patience for bickering than the rest of us.

"Whoa, whoa, whoa," Whitney said, standing up and getting between Chandra and Kimberly. "We are not going to get into petty arguments right now. Remember what happened to this squad the last time we let that happen?"

"Look, all I'm saying is, we have the time. If we're going to do it, we may as well do it now," Tara said. God, she was acting like it was no big deal. Like dyeing my hair was as simple a decision as deciding to breathe.

I swallowed hard and glanced at Chandra, hoping for a little support. Everyone knew she was a bottle blonde. Sometimes I wished she would just grow those roots of hers out already so that I wouldn't be alone in all this platinum hell.

"I'm in," Sage said giddily.

Shocker, I thought. Everyone eyed me expectantly, wondering if I would cave. All it made me want to do was fight back.

"I don't know, Tara," I said in a super-sweet tone. "We didn't dye my hair the night before regionals. I mean, won't it kill our luck?"

Silence. Tara's mouth dropped open slightly, but nothing came out.

Gotcha! I thought.

Whitney reached toward me and I slapped her five. Tara glared at us and let out an exasperated groan. She sat down hard on the floor, yanked out her cucumber eye pillow and lay back, her arms crossed firmly over her chest.

Before anyone could say anything else, I got up and flipped the light switch, dousing us all in darkness. Case closed. For now.

• • •

By the time I "woke up" the following morning, I was physically exhausted. I wasn't convinced that I had slept at all,

57

actually. Between nationals nervousness, Daniel-obsessing, and the whole blonde thing, my mind had been racing all night. Plus, Chandra had snored on and off throughout the wee morning hours, Sage had insisted we leave the bathroom light on, and sometime around midnight Autumn had shouted something in her sleep about rainbow rabbits in springtime. What the heck was that about?

I thought about calling Jordan for a quick pep talk, but at this indecent hour, I knew she was still asleep. I yawned hugely as I sat up in my sleeping bag, wishing I was in Snoozeland with her.

Of course, I couldn't be groggy for long. We were going to nationals today! Eventually the jitters and excitement had to snuff the tiredness. Chandra's mother was in the kitchen at dawn, making the most yummy-smelling concoction of foods I had ever, well, smelled. Soon everyone was yawning, stretching and drooling for the coffee, bacon, frittatas and pancakes we had coming our way. The sun was shining, and as I took my turn in the bathroom to wash my face, I resolved not to think about Daniel or hair dye anymore. It was time to focus on the task at hand. This was nationals, people. I had to be the best cheerleader I could possibly be.

"Let's sit out on the patio," I suggested to Mindy when I emerged all fresh-faced and minty-breathed. "I could use some fresh air."

"Sounds good," she replied. "Save me a seat."

Some of the girls were already chowing down in the kitchen and they all shouted greetings as I walked by. Hyper city. Sage was once again gabbing with Lindsey and I purposely tuned them out. If she was talking about Daniel again, I did *not* want to know. I was paranoid enough already. I headed outside and took a chair next to Autumn at the glass-topped patio table. Birds were chirping in the palm trees and I leaned back and took a long, deep breath.

"You're such a morning person," Phoebe said grumpily as she plopped down across from me. She took a swig of her coffee and rested her chin on her hand. "If you start humming or something, I may have to kill you."

"No humming, got it," I said, grabbing a couple of pancakes from the platter in the center of the table.

"More juice, anyone?" Chandra asked, emerging from the kitchen with a carton of Tropicana. "Or we've got tomato, apple, pineapple."

"I'll take some, thanks," I said. Chandra poured me a cup and set it in front of me.

"Let me know if you guys need anything else," she said perkily.

"Okay, I may have to kill her too," Phoebe said, slumping further.

"Who knew Chandra was the hostess with the mostest?" I said. I doused my pancakes with syrup and took a slug of juice. There is nothing I love better than a big, sugary breakfast.

"Well, she does help out with her mom's catering company," Autumn said. "I think this morning she just flipped into 'the customer is always right' mode."

"Or maybe it's just 'I want to be captain next year' mode," Erin said, pulling her thick blonde braid over her shoulder as she grabbed a few pancakes. She ripped a chunk off of one and stuffed it into her mouth. "She's kissing butt."

I stopped chewing and looked at her. *Geez. Tell us how you really feel.*

"What?" she asked, brown eyes wide. "You don't think she's hosting all these sleepovers and having her mom whip up these incredible meals and everything for a reason?"

"Erin!" Autumn hissed, glancing over her shoulder. "We're not supposed to be talking about this."

"Whatever," Erin said. "You know you're all thinking about it. Everyone at this table has been trying to figure out who they're gonna vote for ever since the props box."

"Not me, really," I said. "Are you gonna run?"

"Maybe," Erin said with a shrug, popping a strawberry into her mouth.

"So what's your platform?" Phoebe asked with a yawn. "You want to be captain, you gotta have a platform."

"Leadership ability," Erin said. "Jaimee's too wishy-washy. I love the girl, but it takes her fifteen minutes to decide on a lip gloss. And Chandra is cool, but I don't know if she could really take charge. *I* would take charge."

"Take charge? What ever happened to democracy?" Autumn asked. "Personally I think we've been suffering under a dictatorship for long enough."

Felice snorted a laugh from behind her book.

"No offense," Autumn said to Phoebe, one of Tara's closest friends.

"Not a problem," Phoebe replied, yawning again.

"But it works, doesn't it?" Erin asked. "We *are* going to nationals."

No one could argue with that point. Although I wasn't entirely sure that it was Tara's leadership skills that had gotten us there. Whenever the going got tough, Tara seemed to blame everyone around her but herself.

"Well, I'm going to go get some more coffee," Erin said, standing. "Anybody want some?"

Phoebe silently held up her drained mug and Erin snatched it as she went by. I looked at Autumn and placed my fork down on my plate.

"That was brave," I said.

"Well, it's how I feel," Autumn replied. "And if you can't tell people how you feel, you're just an empty shell."

"Do you really think Chandra wants to be captain?"

"Oh, I know she does," Autumn said. "She told me at the beginning of the season. Looks like we have a three-way race on our hands."

She grabbed a piece of mango and sat back, pressing her shin against the side of the table. The bells on her anklet chimed as she moved. Together we watched the scene in the kitchen through the glass sliding doors. Chandra grabbed the coffee carafe out of Erin's hands and insisted on pouring the coffee *for* her. Meanwhile, from across the room, Jaimee watched them both with interest, even as she babbled on to the other squad members at her table.

"Maybe we should scrap the gymnastics coach and hire a meditation guru instead," Autumn said. "Because eventually, this is going to get ugly."

Inside the kitchen Erin and Chandra smiled at each other falsely and Jaimee, observing them, opened up her spiral journal and scribbled something down. I had a feeling Autumn's instincts were dead-on. I just hoped the ugliness would hold off until after nationals. Otherwise Tara was going to show us all just what a dictator she could be.

"Hey! How my girls doing?" Coach Holmes called out with a bright smile. A few girls cheered in reply. She was waiting in the school parking lot by the open door of our state-of-the-art bus, looking very Beyoncé-on-vacay. Her dyed-blonde hair was back in a high ponytail and she was wearing a light blue track suit. Her dark skin glowed and her eyes were bright. If she were anyone else, I would have thought *Red Bull for breakfast*, but Coach Holmes was pretty much always on.

Steven was there as well with his camera at the ready. He was wearing a brand-spanking-new Crabs baseball cap and a red polo shirt.

"Nice hat," I told him.

"Figured I'd get with the program. Show a little school spirit," he said, touching the bill. "Smile!"

I grinned, grabbed Mindy around the neck and pulled her toward me. He snapped the picture and checked the screen. "Nice one!"

A purple spot floated across my vision and Mindy blinked a few times. I just hoped Steven wasn't too snap-happy for the next few days. Stunts would be problematic if we were all flash-blind.

"You really need the flash in this weather?" I asked, squinting toward the sun.

"Oh, oops," he said with an apologetic shrug. "Probably not."

I was glad to see he wasn't acting all-knowing, all the time. Maybe having him on this trip with us wouldn't be *so* bad.

"Morning, Coach," I said as everyone lined up to stash their suitcases under the bus. Nationals were held every year right here in Florida, so we only had to endure a short-ish bus ride. Other squads were being flown in from all over the country.

"Annisa! Looking good!" Coach said in reply, slapping me on the shoulder.

I glanced down at my outfit—crisp white T-shirt over light blue shorts with a yellow SDH megaphone on the right leg. Actually, I looked pretty much like everyone else on the squad. Coach had insisted that we arrive at nationals looking uniform, and while we were there, we were supposed to show our Sand Dune pride by dressing alike at all times except at dinner. We each had a half dozen similar outfits stashed in our bags.

"Phoebe! Where's the energy?" Coach asked as Phoebe hoisted her bag into the cargo hold using two hands.

"Talk to me around 10 A.M., Coach," Phoebe said bluntly.

Coach Holmes laughed. "All right! Let's get going! Everyone on the bus!" she shouted. "Are we psyched up for nationals?"

"Yeah!" everyone cheered in response. I saw the paunchy bus driver trying not to laugh.

"I *said,* are we psyched up for nationals?" Coach repeated at the top of her lungs.

64

"YEAH!" everyone shouted again, this time adding some whoops and hollers.

"So let's go!" Coach shouted.

We started up the steps into the bus and I checked my cell phone quickly, just to see if I had missed a ring. There was nothing. No voice mail. No text messages. No sign of Daniel whatsoever.

"Tara, how many times have I told you to change those to'-up socks?" Coach asked, stopping Tara with her hand before she could board the bus. We all looked down at Tara's ratty feet. The socks were looking almost black around the edges today. "You cannot wear those in the competition."

"I know, Coach," Tara said. "I'm going to wear them *under* my clean ones."

Chandra stuck out her tongue and rolled her eyes back, but at least she didn't have to live with the girl. For some reason Coach had assigned Mindy and me to room with Tara and Phoebe at the hotel. I just hoped Tara kept her feet as far away from me as possible.

"Forget dictator," Erin said in my ear. "Try deranged."

I laughed and stepped up into the bus.

• • •

"You know what I love!?" Sage announced over the din created by sixteen loud voices, several bleeping cell phones and one portable stereo. "I *love* that everyone else we know is in class right now!"

"Omigod, I am *so* happy not to be sitting in health listening to Mr. Marcal's lecture about safe sex," Jaimee said with a fake gag. She, Mindy, Erin and I were all up on our knees, hanging over the backs of our seats so we could chat with the rest of the team. Steven sat in the very back corner, alternately snapping pictures and taking notes.

"Seriously. I swear the last time that guy got some, the condom hadn't even been invented," Whitney put in.

"Is it just me, or does he start to sweat profusely when anyone mentions the word *vagina*?" Autumn asked as she wove a tiny braid into her ponytail. "It's a functional part of the human *body*. He's a *health* teacher."

"Ladies! Have some respect for those of us who have dedicated our lives to your education!" Coach Holmes called out from the front of the bus.

"Or our *mis*education," Tara said quietly, rolling her eyes.

"Tara!" Coach shouted.

"Gum, anyone?" Mindy asked, offering a pack. I grabbed a stick as Erin's cell phone rang. She flipped it open and slid down in her seat.

"Hey, baby," she said with a smile.

"Carlos," Jaimee said knowingly.

Erin had been dating Carlos Verde since before I moved to Sand Dune. Aside from Tara and Bobby Goow, they were definitely the most solid couple I knew of. As she cupped her hand over her mouth and whispered sweet somethings into her phone, I pulled mine out and checked for messages one more time. My heart skipped a beat when I saw the text icon flashing. Had Daniel finally sent me a good-luck message? Or maybe Jordan?

I hit the button and sighed. The text was from my brother, Gabe.

Gabe: break a leg! will see u there! am home now. got any gel around here?

66

Gel? Like *hair* gel? Since when did Gabe use products? Sometimes I was unsure of whether he even owned shampoo. I wrote him back quickly.

Annisa: gel in vanity table drawer. don't use 4 anything weird!!!

I hit SEND and then quickly turned off my phone, sick of the blank screen mocking me. As Mindy and the others took up the topic of carbs vs. protein, I sat down in my seat and stared out the window at the passing scenery. Nothing but swamps and cows as far as the eye could see.

Are you my boyfriend or what? my voice played in my head.

I groaned and put my hand over my eyes, sinking lower in my seat.

Are you my boyfriend or what?

I took a deep breath. All right. I was fine. I just had to think about something else. Nationals. We were going to nationals. I started to play the routine over in my head. Music starts. Pop up. First basket toss. Toe-touch. Come down. Formation change. Dance sequence and—

Are you my boyfriend or what?

Argh! Suddenly I saw the present me sitting behind the past me in Daniel's car, slapping my own hand over my mouth from behind before I could say those stupid words. Why couldn't I have just kept my yap shut? Why couldn't I ever think before I spoke?

"Hey!" Steven dropped into the seat next to me. I looked up, confused. I hadn't even noticed Mindy moving across the aisle. "Everything okay?" he asked.

"That depends," I said, glancing at the tape recorder in his hand.

He flushed slightly and pocketed it. "Speak freely."

I looked at his open, concerned face and for a moment thought about telling him what had happened with Daniel. After all, he was a guy. Maybe he could give me the male perspective on things. But I had just chided myself for never keeping my mouth shut. Maybe, for once, I should give it a try.

"I guess I'm just nervous," I told him, using my fingertip to trace the bus company's logo on the back of the seat in front of me.

"Want to borrow my iPod?" Steven asked, producing a sleek silver version from an inner pocket of his denim jacket. "I uploaded the entire Beatles catalog onto it last night. They're actually pretty good."

"Hello? That's the understatement of the year," I said.

"Okay, I get it now!" Steven said with a laugh. "So do you want it?"

"That's okay. Maybe later," I said. "I don't think I'm in a musical mood right now."

"Well, I still have some more questions for your interview," Steven said. "Let's get that out of the way."

I took a deep breath and let it out slowly. "Yeah, okay, sure." *As long as there are no more questions about a certain football player that I'm not going to think about anymore.*

Steven took out his tape recorder again. "Ready?"

"Ready."

He hit RECORD. "Okay, so we were talking about your best friend Jordan and your squad back in New Jersey," Steven said. "What do you think they would say if they could see you right now?"

I looked down at myself and laughed. "They'd probably think I'd joined a cult or something."

"Really?"

"Well, most of them would," I replied, pushing myself up a little. "We were a team, but everyone was a little bit apathetic about it. Like they were afraid to be *too* into it because being too into it would make it uncool or something."

"What about you?" Steven asked.

"Oh, I was into it," I said. "So was Jordan. We had all these plans for when we were seniors. We were going to get new uniforms and try to recruit from the gymnastics team and definitely try to compete."

"Cool," Steven said. "So you're a take-action kind of person."

"I guess," I said. *Sometimes,* I added silently.

But I knew that if Jordan and I were together and leading the squad, we definitely would have changed things. Working together, we were fairly unstoppable.

I sighed, overcome with sudden nostalgia. Jordan and I had spent an entire summer afternoon poring over cheerleading catalogs, picking out little vests and minis to replace the ages-old sweaters we were forced to wear. When I had e-mailed her a picture of the Sand Dune squad, she had pointed out that we had almost the exact same uniforms she and I had coveted, just in different colors. Suddenly I missed Jordan so much, I could feel my heart trying to tear its way out of my chest.

"I have to make a phone call," I said, taking my phone out again.

"Jordan?" Steven asked.

"Very observant of you, reporter man," I said with a smirk.

He grinned and got up to give me a little privacy. I noticed that my hand was actually quaking a little as I powered up the phone. I had to talk to Jordan about Daniel. Enough was enough already. Jordan would have some kind of advice to make me feel better, like she always did. Making me feel better was practically her calling.

Finally my phone gave that little trill to tell me it was ready. I was about to hit Jordan's speed-dial button when the message NO SIGNAL flashed onto the screen.

I jumped up and turned around. I would not be so easily deterred.

"Anyone have a signal right now?" I asked. "Well, a signal and national service?"

"I have national," Whitney said. "But my battery's toast."

"Anyone else?" I asked.

There were a bunch of shrugs and nos. It looked like I was going to have to wait until we got to the hotel for my comfort call.

"Uh . . . Sage? Hello?" Whitney said, waving her hand.

"What?" Sage asked blankly.

"Lend the girl your phone!" Whitney replied.

"Uh! Fine!" Sage replied. She made a big show of pulling out her phone and flopped her arm dramatically as she handed it over. "Just don't gab all day," she said—the first words she had spoken to me since the obnoxiousness of last night. "I need to keep the line open."

We get it, I thought. *You have a mystery man. Go you.*

"Thanks," I said sweetly. Then I sat back and dialed Jordan's number. It rang twice. Three times. Then her voice mail picked up. My spirits drooped.

"Hey. It's Jordan. Hit me."

"Hey, Jor, it's me," I said. "Call me back on my cell as soon as you get this. It's a code red. Miss you."

I hung up and let my hand drop to my lap. So much for that. I glanced down at the phone and saw that Sage had chosen a little butterfly animation as a screensaver. Beneath the flapping wings, the menu button was already highlighted.

My heart skipped a beat as a wicked idea formed. I glanced over my shoulder and saw that everyone was engaged in a huge debate over the MTV vs. Fuse issue, with Sage at the center.

Don't do it, the little angel on my shoulder intoned. *Respect the girl's privacy.*

Come on, it's no big deal, the devil on the other shoulder prodded. *You know you're dying to know. And besides, she deserves it after her stunning rudeness last night.*

I don't know if it was because I was in a bad mood or because Sage had been so bitchy from day one or because of how smug she was acting over her man, but for once, I listened to the little devil. I had to know who her secret crush was.

Heart pounding, I hit the menu button. I scrolled to INCOMING CALLS. I hit the green button and there, right in front of me, was the list of numbers that had called Sage's cell in the last twenty-four hours.

Instantly, the entire bus went into a freefall, everyone

71

screaming and crying and clutching their seats for dear life around me.

The caller ID read, DANIEL HOME.

Last night, at exactly 8:04 P.M., approximately the time Whitney and Phoebe had left on the M&M run, Sage had received a call from Daniel Healy.

I was going to kill her. No, I was going to kill him. No, I was going to kill them both!

Daniel Home.

Daniel Home.

Daniel Home.

I couldn't stop staring at it. If I stopped staring at it, I was going to fling it out the window.

Okay, I had to breathe.

I wasn't really going to kill anyone. Not really. But you can understand that my brain wasn't exactly functioning properly at that moment. Daniel had called Sage. *Daniel* had called *Sage.* Here I had been waiting for a call or a text or a freakin' *smoke signal* from him all night and day and he was calling Sage and making her go all squealy.

The bus driver pressed the brakes as we hit some traffic and my stomach lurched dangerously. I reached up, opened the latches on the tinted bus window and used my shoulder to shove it open. Then I dropped back into my seat and leaned toward the aisle.

"Mindy!" I loud-whispered, gasping for air.

She glanced over at me and, not surprisingly, appeared rather concerned when she saw my face. Sage was still engaged in her oratory about her love for Quddus and she didn't even bat any of her ridiculously long eyelashes as Mindy broke away and settled in next to me.

"What's wrong?" she asked. "You look like you just swallowed a bug."

"Thanks for that visual," I said, grimacing. "Look at this."

I showed her the evidence and it took a moment for the significance to register. When it did, her face turned to granite.

"Daniel?" she said.

"Tell me there is a logical explanation," I replied.

Mindy stared at the seat back in front of her for a moment. "Okay! Okay! He could have called her for any reason," she said, suddenly animated. "Maybe he just wanted to wish her luck on the competition."

That idea was like a baseball bat to the gut. After all, a good-luck call was all I had been looking for and I still hadn't gotten one. But I supposed that a quick break-a-leg call to his ex for old-times' sake was better than him calling to profess his undying love.

"Or . . . or maybe he called about homework," Mindy spitballed. "Or! Maybe he found something of hers that he's had since their breakup and wants to give it back!"

She looked particularly proud of that idea. And I have to admit, it was a pretty tempting scenario.

"But she was so giddy when she came back into the room last night," I reminded Mindy. "She wouldn't have been giddy if he had told her he wanted to give back her *Miss Congeniality* DVD."

"True. *But* maybe she called somebody back *after* she talked to Daniel and *that's* what made her giddy!" Mindy said triumphantly. "Here. Let's see."

74

She took the phone out of my hand and hit a few buttons. She must have really wanted to clear Daniel and make me feel better. Invading someone's privacy was not a Mindy type of thing to do. Actually, it wasn't usually an Annisa type of thing to do, and you best believe I was already regretting it. Stupid shoulder devil.

"Darn. Her outgoing call list is empty," Mindy whispered. "She must have erased it."

"I can't believe she's talking to Daniel, whatever they're talking about," I said quietly. "He hasn't called me, but he's called her."

"Okay, look," Mindy said, handing back the phone and turning in her seat. Her blue eyes were earnest as she looked me in the eye and grabbed my wrists. "This doesn't mean anything. Daniel really likes you, okay? It's totally obvious to the world."

"Really?" I asked.

"He walks you to school every single day," she said. "He waits for you outside of class. He even arm-wrestled Carlos for the last chocolate cupcake at lunch that day to cheer you up after your math test."

I smiled. There really was some solid evidence in my favor here. Suddenly I was very glad that it was Mindy on this trip with me and not Bethany. Bethany would have taken one look at the cell phone, gotten up and hung Sage out the bus window by her ankles. Or possibly just shouted at her until she cried. Either way, Mindy's pep talk was a lot more productive. Of course, Jordan would have been my first choice, but she was probably in biology class right about now. I don't know what I had been thinking trying her cell phone on a school day, but maybe she would call me back at lunch. I hoped.

"We're about five minutes away from nationals," Mindy said, glancing out the window at the heavy traffic. "You have to give Sage the benefit of the doubt. For the team."

I took a deep breath. Mindy was right. I had to shelve all these negative thoughts or I was going to be putting the *poop* in *party pooper*.

"Hello? Could you quit bogarting my phone already?" Sage said, coming up the aisle toward us. "I'm waiting for a call."

I'll bet you are, I thought.

I handed her the phone without a word and turned to look out the window in an effort to hide my sour expression. The bus was just pulling into the parking lot of the Regency Palm Hotel and Convention Center where nationals were being held. The place was total mayhem. I had to get a grip so that I wouldn't let the squad down. This was, after all, the biggest event of our lives.

Of course, if we're being fair here, Sage was the one who was really letting *me* down, right? I mean, taking secret calls from my maybe-boyfriend? And how about all those squad mates who wanted me to dye my hair? Why did it sometimes seem like I was the only one making sacrifices around here?

"You okay?" Mindy asked.

The air brakes squealed and everyone popped up from their seats in excitement. Somewhere outside the window a squad was chanting, "S-P-I-R-I-T! We've got the spirit! Let's hear it!"

I forced a smile. "Fine," I said. "Let's get this party started."

• • •

"Okay, whoa," Jaimee said as she stepped off the bus.

"I'll second that exclamation," I said, dropping to the ground next to her.

Gradually the entire squad lined up next to the bus and took it all in. The cars and buses decked out in spray paint and streamers. The squads in full uniform stunting in the middle of the parking lot. The screaming group of girls in red and blue colliding with another group in brown and orange, everyone hugging and kissing and screeching with uninhibited delight at their reunion. Horns honked. Some lady on a bullhorn tried to instill order. A raccoon mascot raced by us and executed a cartwheel before raising his fists in triumph and tearing off.

"Toto, we're definitely not in Sand Dune anymore," Chandra said.

"All right, girls. Let's stop gaping," Tara said, clapping her hands together. "We don't want to look like a bunch of tourists who don't belong, do we?"

A troop of younger girls, undoubtedly from the junior division, trailed by us, holding hands to make a chain. They all had glittery orange and purple stars stuck just under their bottom lashes and their ponytails all looked like they were the exact same length with the exact same curl. Though, I was quick to note, they were a multitude of colors.

"Peppy Ponys," Whitney said.

"Huh?" I asked.

"They're a leader in fake cheer hair," Whitney replied.

"See? I'm not the only one who wants to look uniform," Tara said as we all started to unload our bags.

"At least a Peppy Pony isn't permanent," I replied.

"Say that three times fast," Erin joked.

"Look," Tara began. "All I'm trying to do is—"

"Omigosh, you guys!" Mindy whispered. "Isn't that . . . ?"

We all turned around to find a crowd of girls walking up the hotel's front pathway toward the automatic sliding doors. They were dressed in black shorts and red hoodies, their hair pulled back with perfect red ribbons. Each of them toted a matching black-and-red duffel bag with a paw print on the side and their names embroidered beneath the emblem. Their chins were held high as they walked, talking in hushed tones as they surveyed the other squads. They carried themselves like total veterans.

I instantly wanted to take them down. Hard.

"The Black Bears," Tara said through her teeth.

The drop-dead-gorgeous Asian girl at the front of the squad glanced our way as they floated by. Her dark eyes flicked up and down over our group and she gave us a little half smile that dripped with condescension. Steven snapped her picture.

"What are you doing?" I asked him. "They're the enemy!"

"Hey! It's not a story if I don't get all sides," he said.

"Come on, girls," Coach Holmes said, knocking us out of our daze. "Let's get checked in."

We were sluggish as we hefted our bags and headed for the hotel. Just like that, the Black Bears had taken some of the wind out of our sails. But I couldn't help it. I had never seen that many pairs of such muscular legs in one place in my life! And they just *oozed* confidence. Like they already had the trophy in their hands.

"Now I'm depressed," Phoebe said, popping open a Red Bull as we walked.

"Tell me about it," Erin added.

Chandra took out a Kit Kat and crunched into it.

I wanted to add my laments, but something inside of me paused. This was no time for self-pity. We were at a national *cheer*leading competition. And we deserved to be here just as much as anyone else. Besides, if I didn't start reclaiming my positive attitude soon, there was no telling if it would ever come back. I was getting sick of feeling so negative.

"Come on, you guys!" I said, skipping up to the front of the line. "We beat some of the best teams in Florida to get here! We beat the West Wind Dolphins!"

They gave me a few half-hearted yeahs.

I rolled my eyes. "What kind of spirit is that? Chandra! Where are the lungs of steel?"

Chandra crumpled her Kit Kat wrapper. "Yeah!" she shouted, getting into it. "We're the Mighty Fighting Sand Dune Crabs! Let's hear it! SDH! SDH! SDH!"

Gradually everyone joined her and Coach Holmes laughed. Now *this* was more like it. Maybe if I could just forget about Sage's existence entirely, this trip could be kind of fun!

"Annisa! Hey! Neece!"

Somewhere, through all the cheering, I heard someone shouting my name. Confused, I turned around and scanned the crowd of girls coming in behind us. Nothing. I looked down the line of buses and vans waiting to unload. Nothing. Was I hearing things now?

"Over here, you reject!"

Wait a minute . . .

"Jordan?" I cried, spinning around.

And there she was, stepping out of an airport shuttle, grinning from ear to ear. Her familiar curly brown hair stuck out at every angle and a pair of huge hoops dangled from her ears. It was really her. Jordan was here! The very person I was aching to talk to with every fiber of my being. She was really here!

"Surprise!" Jordan shouted.

I raced toward her and threw myself into her arms. You would have thought we were a couple reuniting after World War II.

"What are you doing here?" I asked.

"Whaddup, Goober?"

That was when I realized that Jordan wasn't alone. The only person who had ever called me Goober and gotten away with it was none other than the infamous Gia Kistrakis. I stepped away from a grinning Jordan and saw that the entire Northwood High Beavers cheerleading squad was descending from the shuttle behind her.

"What are you guys doing here?" I asked, clinging to Jordan.

"Surprise!" she said giddily.

"*How* did you keep this a secret?" I demanded.

Jordan shrugged, grinning. "I am just that good."

Gia lit up a cigarette and Beaver captain Becca Richardson grabbed it out of her hand, crushing it under the toe of her black leather boot.

"What the hell?" Gia snapped, whipping her dark red hair off her face as the wind kicked up. She was sporting purple eyeliner and had a fading red stamp on the back of her hand. Someone had been partying recently.

"You will not get us disqualified," Becca said, pointing a French-manicured nail at Gia. Ah, Becca Richardson. Her thick, straight, light brown hair hung perfectly flat past her shoulders. She wore expertly faded jeans, a sleek black turtleneck and huge diamond studs in her ears. At Northwood High she was an icon of style. She spent her weekends shopping in New York City with Daddy's credit card and carried herself like a friend-of-Gwyneth. You just knew she was going to walk right out of college one day and into some incredible fashion-mag job where she would be hobnobbing with the rich and famous. She was just born to hobnob.

"No smoking," Becca added. Then she leaned forward and whispered loud enough for all of us to hear, "At least not in public."

Gia snickered as Becca turned and gave me a huge hug. I could hardly breathe. Becca Richardson was hugging me. Becca Richardson—the coolest girl I had ever known. We're talking confident, beautiful, unfazeable. Back in Jersey, if she had even said "hey" to me or snapped her gum in my general direction, I would have been kvelling for hours. I'm not proud to admit it, but I pretty much worshipped the ground she walked on. Like when I got myself into a really embarrassing situation, sometimes I thought, "What would Becca Richardson do?" Of course, the answer was usually, "She never would have gotten into the situation in the first place."

"It's good to see you, Annisa!" she said, air-kissing me. "The squad is not the same without you!"

Wow. I mean, seriously. Wow.

"I don't get it," I said, feeling light-headed. "You guys are here to compete?"

Not to take anything away from my old squad, but we had never been what you might call "athletic." Or "motivated." Or "organized." We pretty much just had fun.

"Yeah, well, the antiquated Board of Ed was talking about taking the 'sport' status away from the squad. They were going to revoke our varsity letters and our jackets and everything," Becca said, folding her arms over her chest as some of the other squad members came by to say hello. I noticed that the Northwood High Beavers had *not* dressed alike for their nationals arrival. Not that I was surprised.

"You're kidding," I said. "That's so moronic."

"Preachin' to the choir," Gia said.

Our squad may have been unmotivated, but there wasn't a team at Northwood High that *didn't* suck. Why not take the varsity letters away from the 0-and-9 football team? Or the soccer team who had recorded its only win last year when the other squad got lost on the way to our school and had to forfeit?

"So anyway, Coach Martinez struck a deal with them," Jordan said. "If we started competing, we would be able to keep our sport status."

"So we signed up for the first regional competition that came around," Gia said, snapping her gum. "After we recruited a few gymnasts and basically practiced our asses off."

She lifted her long sweater to show me her butt. I swear she had lost at least twenty pounds since I had last seen her.

"Sweet," I said.

"Ain't it?" she replied.

"So by the time the competition rolled around, half the state was flattened with this evil flu. We were the only healthy ones there," Becca continued.

"We won in a landslide!" Jordan said giddily.

"You guys even get the flu down here?" Gia asked, squinting up at the sun.

"Not so far," I said. "Omigod, Jordan! How could you not tell me any of this?"

"Well, I never thought we'd actually win, obviously," Jordan said. Gia backhanded her across the shoulder. "OW! Neither did you!" Jordan whined. "Anyway, besides, you were on a *real* competition squad," she told me, eyeing Gia warily. "I guess I just felt kind of weird mentioning it."

I blinked. Huh? Since when could Jordan not tell me stuff? Especially good stuff?

Just then I noticed something out of the corner of my eye and instinctively raised my hand. Sure enough, it was Steven Schwinn, snapping pictures. He *needs* to move to L.A. and get his stalkerazzi card. Stat.

"Yo, Peter Parker, take a pill," Gia said, stepping so close to him, she blocked his entire lens.

"You must be Gia," he said, having the sense to look nervous.

"My reputation precedes me," Gia said with a smile.

"This is Steven," I said, lifting a hand. "He's doing a story for my school paper about the competition."

"So are those your friends?" Jordan asked, looking past me.

I turned around and gulped. The entire Sand Dune High

cheerleading squad was standing in a clump, some looking restless, others blatantly staring the Beavers down. I could only imagine what the Crabs thought of Becca and her ragtag-looking squad. Tara glanced pointedly at her watch.

"Yep."

"Nice outfits," Becca said, earning a laugh from the Beavers around her.

I blushed painfully. Suddenly I felt as if I were in the middle of a bad *West Side Story* remake. I looked from one glowering squad to the other and back again, imagining them decked out in cheerleading uniforms and leather jackets, slowly approaching one another, ready to rumble. Only instead of blades they had poms. And instead of pipes they wielded megaphones.

"Annisa? You coming?" Whitney called finally.

"I guess I should go," I said to Jordan, giving her another squeeze. "I am *so* glad to see you. We have to talk later," I added.

"Everything okay?" she asked, catching my tone.

"Not really," I said. "But it's better now that you're here."

"Aw!" Gia and Becca intoned, then laughed.

Jordan rolled her eyes. "Catch ya later."

I turned and jogged back to the squad, still giddy and shocked. I couldn't believe the Beavers were actually here. Competing. I felt like I had been drop-kicked into an alternate reality.

"Who were those freaks?" Sage asked. So predictable.

"That's my old team," I replied calmly.

Everyone cracked up. "You're kidding. *Them*?" Tara asked. "What are they, just here to observe?"

"I didn't know Gothland had cheerleaders," Phoebe joked.

"Their class-trip bus probably took a wrong turn at the third landfill," Sage added.

My face burned. "Ha ha, you guys. Don't knock New Jersey until you've been there. It's actually really pretty."

"Whatever you say," Tara replied. "I bet those chicks and their hairspray are personally responsible for the hole in the ozone layer."

"And did you check the eyeliner?" Kimberly added. "That one girl looks like a straight-up ho."

"Kimberly!" Mindy admonished.

I felt like I had been slapped. "You guys! You're talking about my friends!"

"Yeah, guys. Back off," Autumn said. "How would you like it if you had to join another squad and then *they* all talked smack about *us*?"

There was total silence. I wasn't sure if people were agreeing with her or trying to figure out what the heck she had just said.

"Have a little maturity, you guys," Autumn added finally.

Phoebe looked at me, chagrined. "Sorry, Annisa. That was rude. I take it back."

"Yeah, my bad," Kimberly added.

"It's okay," I replied.

Although it wasn't. Not really. I mean, if that was what they thought about the Beavers, did that mean they thought the same things about me?

"They're her friends. She should be able to talk to them if she wants to," Jaimee said with a quick nod. Then she looked at the others. "I mean, unless you guys really don't want her to," she added. "Maybe we should take a vote?"

"On whether I can talk to my best friend?" I exclaimed.

Jaimee bit her lip and shrugged by way of apology.

"I just don't think that we should be fraternizing with the enemy right now. This is nationals, people. We should be acting like a squad," Erin put in, heading for the front door of the hotel.

"Hello, Mini-Tara," Phoebe whispered to me.

"Isn't anyone down with democracy anymore?" Autumn added.

Everyone looked at Chandra as if expecting her to weigh in on the issue. Jaimee had said her piece. Erin had said hers. It seemed it was time for Chandra, our third captain candidate, to say something. Suddenly everything was a campaign issue.

Chandra shrugged. "If you ask me, Annisa can do what she wants. I just want to get to my room."

As we all followed after Erin, a couple of my squad mates looked back at the Beavers, who were trying their best to heft all their bags and winter coats as they straggled toward us. I caught a few giggles and snickers, and was reminded of my first couple of weeks on the squad, back when I was treated like a leper. But I took a deep breath and told myself to ignore it. Nobody was perfect. And besides, things had changed since then . . . right? Now that they knew me, they knew I wasn't some stereotype. I hoped.

"Wait! Stop!" Tara shouted, throwing her arms out.

We all bumped into each other as we tried to bring ourselves up short. Tara looked up through the glass-fronted lobby, where a couple of guys were up on ladders, stringing a huge banner.

"We need to find another way in," she said. "We are not walking under those guys."

"But you're not walking under a *ladder*," Whitney pointed out. "You're walking under a banner."

"Well, tom-*ay*-to, tom-*ah*-to," Tara said, adjusting her shoulder strap. "Let's go."

With that, she walked off around the side of the building to find another entrance. Unbelievable. She may have gotten a little superstition-crazy since regionals, but until recently at least she had kept it to the socks and the hair ribbon. Now, between the cookies and the J. Lo and the sleeping arrangements at the slumber party and the ladder, she was dragging us all down with her. Still, it didn't seem like the right time to start arguing with *El Capitán*. With a sigh and a grumble, we all followed her.

Like I said, nobody's perfect.

• • •

After checking us in, Coach Holmes gathered us all in a corner of the hotel lobby. The whole room was about twelve stories high and topped by a dome of glass. Palm trees, couches and chairs dotted the slick marble floor and every accent from the plant stands to the elevator doors was gold. It kind of looked how I'd imagine ancient Athens to be. Only without all the dudes in togas.

"Okay, everyone," Coach Holmes shouted, shushing our conversations. "Here's your information packet for the duration of our stay."

She handed each of us a sleek red folder with the competition's logo on the front. Inside were several sheets of colorful paper with maps of the hotel and grounds, rules of the competition, a code of conduct and a bunch of other information. Everyone flipped through the pages quickly, trying to take it all in. There was going to be a lot to remember.

I looked around the sunlit lobby and saw the Beavers at the front desk. Coach Martinez had chopped her hair super short and looked kind of modelesque in a slim gray suit. The airy lobby was so full of people and noise I could barely hear what Coach Holmes was saying, but I did hear Gia's cackle of a laugh from all the way across the room. I bit my lip to keep from smiling and tried to pay attention.

"Check it out," Chandra whispered, elbowing me. She pulled out a sheet of orange paper. "We're practicing in Ballroom A with the Southeast High School Lions of Tennessee, the *Northwood High Beavers,* and the *Mecatur High Black Bears.*"

I looked down at the page, dumbstruck. "You've gotta be kidding me."

"Talk about worlds colliding," Chandra joked.

This is going to be interesting, I thought, watching Jordan as she and the others headed for the gilded elevators.

"Okay, ladies, you have an hour and a half of free time," Coach Holmes announced. "Get yourselves settled, then we will meet in the restaurant for lunch. After that we have our first practice, so when you come down to eat, I want all of you to be wearing practice uniform number one. Got it?"

Practice uniform number one. What were we, a crack military unit? I mean, I understood trying to maintain some spirit and unity, but did that mean we had to completely stifle our individuality? Suddenly I got a mental picture of the squad all dressed up in army green, marching around the lobby like sentries as Coach Holmes barked orders.

"All right, everyone. You're dismissed!" Coach told us.

I almost cracked up laughing.

• • •

"Wow! This is pretty nice!" Mindy said as she, Tara, Phoebe and I walked into our room.

It was fairly spacious with two double beds covered in gold comforters. A pullout couch sat in a little alcove near the window and there were two sinks out in front of the bathroom, separated from the shower and toilet by a door. Tara dropped her bags on the first bed and started to unpack. Phoebe grabbed the room service menu and hopped onto the second bed. I guess the seniors got pri when it came to sleeping arrangements.

"I'm gonna hang up some of my stuff," Mindy said.

I joined her at the closet across from the sinks and pulled out my bag of toiletries.

"So, was that Jordan downstairs?" Mindy asked as she unfolded a little flowered sundress from her mini suitcase.

"Yeah. You have to meet her," I said. "I hope we get a chance to hang out."

"I'm sure you will," Mindy replied. "Maybe you should call her and we can all go down to the pool for a while. I bet almost everyone is going to be there."

"I don't know if that's such a good idea," Tara said, joining us. She held up a package of Herbal Essences hair dye. "After all, the box says you shouldn't be exposed to chlorine for at least twenty-four hours."

My jaw pretty much fell off my face. Was she ever going to quit? "Tara, I am not going to dye my hair!"

She crossed her arms over her chest. "You know, I can't believe how unreasonable you're being about this!"

"I can't believe you went out and *bought* this stuff!" I said, grabbing the box out of her hand. "Is *this* what you were doing at the drugstore this morning? I mean, don't I even get to pick out the color that my own hair is going to be?"

"So you *will* do it," Tara said, her eyes lighting up.

"No!" I replied, slapping the box down on the counter.

"Tara, maybe we should drop this for now," Phoebe said, appearing in the open doorway. "Come on. I want to check out the fitness center."

I could have hugged her for saving me. But she had said "we." *We* should drop this. Was she part of the dye-Annisa's-hair club?

Tara blew out a long breath. "Fine," she said. "But this isn't over," she told me, pointing in my direction. "We're going to discuss this later."

"You can discuss all you want," I said. "I am not dyeing my hair!" I shouted as the heavy door slammed behind them. "I don't believe this!"

I dropped onto the edge of the bed and slumped. It felt as if a huge weight were pressing down on my chest. How was I going to get Tara to back off? Couldn't she see what all this blonde-hair talk was doing to me?

"Ignore them," Mindy told me. "Seriously. They can't make you do it."

"She's really serious, though," I said, feeling over-whelmed. "I mean, she *bought* the stuff. Am I going to look like a bad squad member if I don't do it?"

"No," Mindy said firmly. "It's your hair."

"Exactly!" I replied. "What if dyeing it ruins it forever? I'll be in college and my hair will be nuclear orange and nobody will want to go out with me and it'll all be because of Tara Timothy."

Mindy laughed. "I doubt that will happen."

At that moment the phone rang loudly and we both jumped.

"Who's that?" Mindy asked.

"Probably Tara calling from the fitness center to tell me to dye my hair," I said. I turned around, leaned over the expanse of the bed and grabbed the receiver from the nightstand.

"Hello?"

"You turned your phone off."

"Bethany?" I said, shooting Mindy a surprised look.

"Look, I just wanted to tell you that Daniel Healy and I had a little chat this morning and I think from now on he's gonna be all kindsa attentive," Bethany said.

My heart thumped. Now I was seeing Bethany hanging *Daniel* out of a window by his ankles.

"*You* talked to *Daniel*?" I said, standing. Mindy was now totally riveted. Bethany and Daniel weren't exactly simpatico. I wasn't sure if they had ever actually spoken before. "Why, Bethany? What did you do?"

"You'll see," she said, with not a small amount of glee in her voice.

"Bethany, come on!" My pulse started to panic. "What did you say to him?"

"Bye, Jersey!" she replied, using Daniel's nickname for me.

"Bethany!"

But the line was dead.

"What's going on?" Mindy asked.

I jumped across the bed and quickly dialed Bethany's cell number. It went directly to voice mail. I groaned and hung up, my heart slamming into my rib cage. Obviously, Bethany would never actually *hurt* Daniel. (I'm sure she *couldn't*, considering his *slight* advantage in the strength department.) It was that mouth of hers that was dangerous. What if she had said something embarrassing to Daniel? What if he thought I was a total freak who needed my best friend to speak for me?

"Annisa? Are you okay?"

I looked up at Mindy and swallowed hard. "Actually, Mindy, I have no idea."

"Okay, so what you need to do is just put it out of your mind," Mindy said.

"Put it out of my mind," I repeated. Put the vision of Bethany talking to Daniel out of mind. Along with Daniel calling Sage. Sage getting all giddy over said call. Oh, and Tara dyeing my hair while I sleep. "It feels like I'm trying to put a lot out of my mind lately."

"I know, but it's just a couple of days," Mindy said. "Then things can go back to normal."

She slipped her sunglasses on as we stepped out of the elevator and headed through the back door of the hotel. I had called Jordan, who had told us the whole Beaver squad was already on their way to the pool, so we were meeting her there.

"Or abnormal, depending on how you look at it," I said with a smile.

"Exactly," she replied.

"So, okay, change of subject." I said, determined. "I like your suit." She was wearing one of those red, white and blue Tommy Hilfiger bikinis and looking quite the All-American Girl. I was just wearing my standard black two-piece.

"Yours too," she said. "Are you sure you used enough sunscreen?"

"Yes, don't worry," I said, patting my mesh bag full of Neutrogena sunblock, SPF 45. "I will not have a random burn pattern for nationals. Just imagine what that would do to Tara's blood pressure. Ever see one of those cartoons where the cat drinks some hot sauce and his head blows off like a volcano?"

"That's about right," Mindy said with a laugh. "Oh, hey. There are your friends."

We wound our way down the path to the pool, which was centered by a huge rock structure full of waterfalls and caves and a slide. The whole area overlooked the beach and the ocean, where a posse of surfers were taking on the mediocre waves. A few squads had already set up camp at various spots around the pool, including Jordan and the rest of the Beavers, almost all of whom were wearing black suits as well. Everyone was checking out everyone else, trying to size up the competition. I wondered how long it would be before a cat fight broke out.

"Jordan!" I called out, waving.

She leaned to the side, squinting in my direction, and waved back. That was when I saw that Gia, Becca and Maria Rinaldi were all gathered around Steven Schwinn's tape recorder, gabbing away. Steven sat in the center of the group, wearing a pair of Hawaiian-print trunks, listening with rapt attention. His hair was slicked back as if he had just gotten out of the pool and he had a towel draped across his lap.

"Huh. Steven Schwinn's actually pretty cute in a bathing suit," Mindy said.

"I hadn't noticed," I replied, even though I had. How could you not? I mean, those lean muscles were right *there.*

I walked over to him and dropped my bag. "Uh . . . what are you doing?"

"Hey, Annisa," he said. "Or should I call you Goober?" he added in a teasing way.

"Um, I wouldn't," Jordan said.

"Are you doing a story about the squad or just about me?" I asked. "Because to be honest, you're starting to get a little stalkeresque."

"Just trying to get the whole picture," Steven said, gathering up his things. "I was just on my way to find Tara Timothy."

"Try the gym," Mindy suggested.

"And tell her I said hey," I added with blatant sarcasm. I watched him scurry off and blew out a sigh. "That guy is starting to freak me out a little bit. I mean, he's nice and everything, but he's *everywhere*. Does he have a twin I don't know about?" I asked Mindy.

"Apparently he's just good at his job," Mindy said with a shrug. "Don't worry. After the competition we won't have to deal with him anymore."

"Hallelujah," I said.

It seemed like everything was going to settle "after the competition." Had I entered an alternate universe or something? Did nationals exist outside the realms of regular time and space? At this point I was wishing I could just fast-forward to Monday.

"Everyone, this is Mindy," I said. "Mindy, this is everyone."

"Hi," Mindy said, raising a hand.

"Hi," the Beavers chorused.

"Is that Elmo on a motorcycle?" Mindy asked, squinting at Gia's ankle tattoo.

"Yeah. What of it?" Gia shot back.

"Nothing! It's really cute!" Mindy said.

Then she quickly dropped onto a lounge chair and pulled out her *Shape* magazine. I should have warned Mindy that everything out of Gia's mouth sounds belligerent. Well, actually, most of it *is*.

"So, what's going on, Goober?" Gia asked. "How's life in the sun?"

"Pretty good," I replied, sitting down sideways on the end of Jordan's chair. She moved her legs to the side to give me more room. "There was a *slight* period of adjustment, but all is well."

"Try a major period," Jordan added, pulling her unruly hair back in a ponytail.

"Okay, yeah, but everything's cool." Even as I said it, I realized it sounded and felt false. If everything were cool, there wouldn't be a box of Herbal Essences waiting for me back in my room. I wouldn't be jealous of Sage anymore and I wouldn't be getting cryptic phone calls from Bethany Goow. "I still can't believe you guys are here."

"Neither can we," Becca said, tipping her face toward the sun. "I could get used to this." I just hoped *they* were wearing sunscreen. Each of the Beavers was pastier than the last.

"And wait till you see our routine," Jordan put in. "You're gonna die."

"I can't wait! You should see this new basket toss we perfected the other day," I told them. "I do a double full in the air. I didn't even think that was possible."

Gia whistled, impressed.

"Cool," Jordan said.

"And then there's this sort of square-dancey, hip-hoppy dance sequence—"

"Um, Annisa?" Mindy said from behind me.

"What's up?" I asked.

"It's just . . . maybe you guys shouldn't be talking about the routines, you know?" Mindy said, looking pained. "Before the competition, I mean."

I laughed. "It's not a problem. We can trust these guys."

"Yeah, Blondie, chill," Gia snapped. "Go back to your *Teen Priss* magazine."

Mindy buried her face in her magazine and I turned to Gia. "You don't have to be mean," I said.

"Sorry," Gia said sarcastically, raising her hands in mock surrender.

Suddenly I felt really hot and really uncomfortable. I wanted to say more, but just that one admonishment had taken a lot of effort. I mean, this was Gia Kistrakis. The girl shoplifted from the Northwood Krauser's right in front of the owner's face every other day and he didn't do anything about it. She was scary.

"Check it out," Becca said, lifting her chin.

The Black Bears squad had entered the pool area and were slowly sashaying their way in our direction. They all wore black, red, or black-and-red bathing suits and had matching Mecatur High beach towels. Talk about uniformity. This was taking bonding to a whole new level. Every other squad by the pool had shushed their conversation and watched the Black Bears with awe. They were real celebrities around here.

Once again, the beautiful Asian girl was at the forefront

of their team, her long black hair hanging straight down her back and almost to her butt. She had to be the captain. Her eyes locked with Becca's as she passed us by. For a moment, no one said a word. Then the Black Bears' captain scoffed.

"Looks like they opened up the competition to white trash this year," she said. My heart plummeted like a stone. Gia started to get up, but Becca grabbed her arm and pushed her back down as she rose herself.

"Excuse me," Becca said loudly.

The girl and her squad stopped. She swung her hair over her shoulder and smiled as Becca approached.

"Yes?" she said.

Becca walked over to her with that confident model walk of hers, lifted her arms and shoved the girl right into the pool. The screech could have shattered glass. Limbs flailed everywhere. Her bag flipped over her head and landed on the big hunk of rock in the center of the pool. By the time the girl surfaced again, her hair plastered like a tangled web over her face, Becca had slapped her hands and returned to her seat.

I'd love to say that I was shocked. But that was Becca Richardson. She was the picture of mature sophistication— until someone insulted her.

All the Beavers applauded and cheered as Becca simply lifted her *Elle* magazine and sat back nonchalantly. The Black Bears fished their captain out of the pool and she dropped her saturated beach towel onto the concrete with a thwack. She stormed over to the end of Becca's chair and this time Gia did stand up, squaring her shoulders like a bodyguard. Amazingly the girl didn't even take note of her.

"You are going to regret that," she told Becca.

"Do you mind? You're blocking my sun," Becca replied, turning a page.

The Black Bears' captain narrowed her eyes menacingly before returning to her friends, all of whom gathered around her as they moved to the other end of the pool.

"Wow," I said finally. "I guess we've had our first cat fight."

"Really, Annisa," Becca said, laying her magazine on her legs. "The term *cat fight* is just so tacky."

I smiled. Becca was in rare form.

"Something wrong?" she asked, glancing past me at Mindy.

I turned around. Mindy's skin *was* looking kind of waxy.

"Actually, I have to go," she said, shoving her magazine into her bag. She shot me this betrayed sort of look as she stood up. "I'll see you back at the room."

I felt a little twist in my stomach when Mindy hurried away. She was a by-the-book kind of girl and I knew that she hadn't liked what Becca had just done. I felt bad that she was so uncomfortable, but still, she didn't have to look at *me* like *I* had done something. That was just Becca. I had seen her do worse, believe me.

"No offense, Annisa, but your new friend is a little uptight," Becca said.

"Come on," I said. "She's cool."

"Cool like the rest of your squad?" Gia asked, picking at a toenail. "They got some new definition of *cool* down here?"

I smirked. "They're okay," I said, knowing it would be kind of pointless to launch a debate.

"Please! Annisa, why are you defending them?" Jordan

asked, sliding forward. She sat next to me and leaned toward the other girls. "You guys should have seen the way they treated her when she moved down here. They were like a bunch of cult psychos. But Annisa totally stood up to them," she said, draping her arm over my shoulder and looking at me proudly. "She wanted to be on that squad, so she told them to shove it and did her thing."

"Go on with your bad self," Becca said a little snarkily.

"That's not how it happened *exactly,*" I said, flushing.

"Yes it is!" Jordan said. "They were total bitches. You hated them. Severely."

"They're not that bad," I told her. "A lot of them are my friends now."

"Right," Jordan said with a laugh and an eye roll. "I'll bet."

"They are," I protested, feeling a little impatient.

Jordan's face sort of fell and she stared at me.

"What?" I asked.

"Nothing," she said. "Forget it."

I wanted to press Jordan, but before I had the chance, Becca cut in. "Well, I'm surprised they even let you on the team, considering your hair color."

"Are they really *all* blonde?" Gia asked.

"Yeah, they are. Well, some of them dye it, but yeah," I said with a laugh. "It's funny you say that, though, because they're actually trying to get me to dye my hair for tomorrow."

I tried to laugh it off like it was a big joke, but they all gaped at me like I'd just said my squad wanted me to grow a third nipple.

"What?" I said uncertainly.

"Tell me you're kidding," Becca said finally.

"No. They're pretty serious about it," I said, swallowing a lump in my throat.

"Some friends," Gia said with a scoff. "Conform or die. Do they want you, or is any mindless blonde A-OK?"

The comment stung. Probably because it put into words a lot of the things I had been trying not to think about. All the things I was supposed to be "putting out of my mind."

"You must really miss us," Becca said, sighing.

She had no idea how much. At least that was how I felt at the moment.

"You're not considering it, obviously," Jordan said. "How could they ask you to do that?"

"Maybe they *are* a cult," Gia put in, widening her eyes.

"Annisa, please tell me you're not gonna dye your hair for them," Jordan said. "Promise."

"Don't worry, I'm not," I said, just wishing I had never brought it up in the first place. The gravity of their reactions made me feel even worse about the whole thing. Clearly no one on the Beavers would ever expect anyone else to change so drastically for them.

"It's unbelievable. Why don't you guys just get matching suits like the bitch brigade?" Becca said, glancing at the Black Bears.

"Or you could break out one of those stretching torture things from the Dark Ages so you could all be the same height," Gia said with a chuckle.

Jordan and I laughed and I leaned back on my elbows. "We could all go for lipo and nose jobs together!" I said.

"And order all your clothes from Talbots," Jordan added.

"And hit L.A. Tans for some matching skin tone."

"What about colored contacts?!"

"Omigod, you guys," I said, laughing. "You should have seen what it was like when I first got here. Remember my rhinestone clip? I may as well have been wearing acid-wash jeans."

"What's wrong with acid-wash jeans?" Gia demanded.

There was a brief pause and then everyone cracked up laughing. It was nice to kick back with my old squad—to be able to say whatever I wanted to say. These days Bethany seemed to be the only person I could do that with. Unless, of course, she *had* used something I said to freak Daniel out.

I nudged Jordan with my elbow. "There is so much I need to tell you," I said under my breath.

She nodded. "We're going inside in a little while. We'll get some time alone then."

I smiled and sat back to soak in the sun. I knew that once I got everything off my chest to Jordan, I would feel better. There was no problem that some QT with my bff couldn't fix.

"So, you guys got any Starbucks down here?" Gia asked me as we walked through the back door of the hotel.

"We're in Florida, not Mars," I told her.

I pulled my black, Indian-inspired tunic cover-up over my head as the cold air-conditioning hit my fresh-outta-the-pool skin. Goose bumps popped up all over my arms and legs. Gia had hardly wrung out her hair and clutched a Belmar Beach Bum towel around her wet bod. She was dripping all over the marble floor. Lawsuit, anyone?

"Come on, G. Let's go check out the gift shop," Becca said, slipping her sunglasses onto the top of her head. She looked, of course, perfect. "I need some gum."

"But I don't have any pockets! Where'm I gonna stash the stuff?" Gia protested, following after her anyway.

Jordan stifled a laugh as the two older girls moved off, Becca floating along, Gia trudging in her wake. "I swear that girl is going to detox while we're here," Jordan said. "No smoking, no drinking, no shoplifting . . . "

"Let's just hope she doesn't get the shakes in the middle of one of your stunts," I joked.

We walked down the hall, flanked by the salon/spa and gym on one side and the gift shop on the other. Inside the salon a couple of women in CHEER MOM T-shirts flipped through *In Touch* magazine, waiting for their appointments. A pair of younger girls in matching outfits walked out of the gift shop, tearing into ice cream sandwiches. As Jordan and I entered the lobby by the elevators, I took a deep breath. I loved hotels. It always amazed me how they constantly smelled so clean and fresh when thousands of people traipsed through there every day. I loved how everything felt new and exotic and the fact that you got a brand-new soap every single day. If I hadn't been due at lunch in half an hour, I would *definitely* have been exploring the rest of the resort.

"So, you want to hang out and talk until we have to—"

Suddenly I felt a swoop of surprise and my head and feet traded places. Not literally. I didn't step in one of Gia's puddles. But I did grab Jordan's arm and stop dead in my tracks to keep from falling over.

"What? What's wrong?" Jordan asked.

"Daniel," I said. "And . . . Bethany."

Okay. This was a hidden-camera moment. What the heck was Daniel Healy doing standing at the check-in desk of my hotel, looking so utterly yummy, you could serve him with whipped cream? Was he here to see me or Sage? Why had he called her last night? *Why?* And what was he doing with *Bethany?* And, hello, shouldn't they both be in U.S. history right about now?

"Annisa, you haven't breathed in about fifty seconds," Jordan said.

I gasped in a breath and my lungs hurt.

"*That's* Daniel?" she whispered, pulling me behind a potted palm tree before he could catch me gaping at him. "Damn, girl. He looks even hotter in person than he does in jpeg."

"Tell me about it," I replied.

"So, what's the sitch? Why haven't you thrown yourself into his arms yet?" Jordan asked.

"That's kind of what I wanted to talk to you about before," I told her. "I—"

"Annisa! Hey! Get your butt over here!" Bethany shouted.

I shot Jordan a helpless look. "We've been made."

On shaky knees, I emerged from behind the tree and met Bethany and Daniel at the check-in counter. Bethany's newly dyed jet-black hair was parted down the center and had been worked into two small braids. She was wearing a black turtleneck with red elbow patches and a pair of denim shorts over purple mesh stockings and black boots. Of course, as out of place as she looked among all the cheerleaders, it was Daniel I couldn't take my eyes off of.

"Hey," he said with a smile.

"Hey," I replied. I wiped my hands on my shorts. "Uh, Daniel Healy, Bethany Goow, this is Jordan Trott."

"Shuddup," Bethany said, removing her dark sunglasses. "So you're the Jersey me?"

"I think *you're* the Florida *me*," Jordan corrected.

"Huh. I thought you'd be pastier," Bethany said.

"I thought you'd be more butch," Jordan shot back.

Bethany snorted a laugh. "Hey, did you see all those motorcycles parked out front? I think there might be a gang here somewhere, lying low and getting ready to start a riot in protest of all the cheer."

"You're kidding," Jordan said. "Harleys or Ducatis?"

"Ninjas."

"Shut *up!*"

"Could be a good angle for a story, no?"

107

Suddenly Bethany and Jordan were gabbing like a pair of long-lost soul mates. I smiled as they moved toward the window so Bethany could point out the bikes. See? I *knew* they shared the same brain.

"So . . . um . . . can I talk to you?" Daniel asked me.

Oh. My. God. Was he going to break up with me? Had he actually driven all the way down here to shatter my heart and tell me he was going back to Sage?

"Sure," I said somehow, wondering if he could hear my heart pounding.

He led me over to a pair of cushy chairs near the wall and sat down, placing his Sand Dune High duffel on the floor at his feet. I had no idea what he was about to say to me, I just hoped I didn't barf up any important organs when he said it.

"I guess you're kind of surprised to see me here," he said.

"Kind of," I replied.

"Well, I've been thinking. . . . Actually, Bethany kind of made me think that . . . well . . . "

Oh, man. Here it comes.

"I've been kind of a wuss lately," he said with a sigh.

"What?" *A wuss?*

"What am I saying?" Daniel said, shaking his head. "Look, what I mean is, I'm sick of being so lame and predictable, you know? Like Reliable Boy or something. I figured it was about time for me to do something crazy."

"Like cutting school and coming down here?" I asked.

"Got it in one," Daniel said.

"Go me."

Sweet relief! He wasn't breaking up with me! Can I get a yee-hah?

"Anyway, Bethany just sort of gave me the smack in the

head I needed, I guess," Daniel continued. "So I told her I was coming here and she was all, 'I'll meet you in the parking lot in ten minutes.' Plus, she had the gas money, so . . . "

"Here you are," I said.

"Here I am," he replied.

"She didn't actually smack you in the head, did she?" I asked, biting my lip.

"No. Not in the physical sense," he said with a laugh. "And you know, she freaked me out a little at first, but she's actually pretty cool. Not half as deranged as I thought."

"Huh. Go figure," I said with a smile.

Daniel scooted forward in his seat and lifted one of my hands from the armrest of my chair. He laced his fingers through mine and ran his thumb along the heel of my hand. Swoon!

"So I was hoping I could take you out to dinner tonight," he said. "Maybe, I don't know, celebrate my transition from Reliable Boy to . . ."

"Rebel Boy?" I supplied.

"Yeah."

I couldn't believe it. He was here for me. He had cut class for me. Not for Sage, for little old me.

But still, I couldn't get the image of that incoming call list out of my mind. This time I wasn't going to let myself stew about it. I had to know.

"Daniel, did you call Sage last night?" I blurted.

"What? No," Daniel said. "Why?"

What was I supposed to say? *I snooped into her call list and saw your number there?* Hardly. So instead, I gazed into his eyes and tried to read them. He really did look confused and surprised. I had to believe him. I wanted to believe him.

109

So I did. I could figure out how his number had gotten on her caller ID later. I mean, maybe someone at his house had misdialed. It was always possible, right?

"Nothing. Forget I asked," I said. Bethany and Jordan walked over, probably sensing it was safe now that Daniel was holding my hand. "Anyway, I'd love to go to dinner, but I can't. I'm supposed to eat all my meals with the squad while I'm here."

"Oh, please!" Jordan said, plopping down on the other armrest. "You can miss one dinner with the Blonde Gestapo. What's going to happen?"

"Tara Timothy could murder me," I replied.

"Your soul, maybe. But she would never actually *kill* you and risk getting all bloodstained," Bethany said. "Unless she used pills. . . . "

We all gaped at Bethany for a second. Then Jordan turned to me. "Seriously though, what are they going to do to you? Not let you compete? If you don't, then none of them can."

She kind of had a point. Tara and Coach could yell at me, but it wasn't like either one of them was going to throw me off the squad. I hated getting yelled at, but Daniel had cut out of school to come down here and be with me. The least I could do in return was cut out of one meal. It wasn't like I would be missing a *practice*. And besides, consequences weren't always as bad as I imagined they would be. I had pre-panicked about a million times in my life and then nothing had happened. I always felt like an idiot for wasting all that time worrying. Maybe it was time for me to take a chance.

"You know what? You're right," I said. I grinned at Daniel

and squeezed his hand. "Meet me at room 1022 at seven o'clock."

"Cool," Daniel said. He looked so pleased, it made my heart spin. "I guess I'll go get checked in. Bobby, Christopher and Carlos are meeting me down here later. I should probably hide the room-service menu and anything that could be used as a funnel."

"Good luck with that," Bethany said, slapping him on the back as he stood. "Now get the hell out of here so we can have some girl time."

Daniel looked at her dubiously.

"Dude, I *am* a girl," she said, tucking her chin and putting her arms out.

"Whatever you say," he joked.

We all watched him go and I knew that Jordan was checking out his butt. Who could blame her?

"So, how cool am I?" Bethany said once Daniel was out of earshot.

"The coolest!" I said, giving her a huge hug. "I cannot believe you got him down here. One day you're going to have to tell me what you said."

"Maybe you'll read about it on sucks-to-be-us.com," she replied.

"Um, please no," I said with a laugh. "But seriously, thank you."

I turned around, all grins, and saw Jordan hovering there, pretending to study the floral print on the chair. A pit of awkwardness opened inside of me and warmed my entire body. Had I just called Bethany the coolest right in front of Jordan? What was wrong with me?

"So, you guys want to show me around this place or what?" Bethany said, patting her laptop bag. "Now that I'm here, I think I'll do a little exposé of my own."

"Actually, we have lunch soon," Jordan said, checking her watch.

"That's right! And then practice," I said. "What are you going to do all day?"

Just then the front door to the lobby opened and a troop of ESPN crew guys in baggy jeans and skintight T-shirts walked through, carrying electrical equipment and huge lighting stands. They were all older and chiseled and they laughed and joked, checking out some of the squads that were lounging around or going over schedules. Bethany eyed them up and down and smirked.

"Oh, I think I can find *something* to do while you melt your brain with the blah-rahs," she said.

We all laughed as one of the guys craned his head around to check out a gorgeous redhead and tripped himself. The awkward moment had thankfully passed.

"Come on," Jordan said. "We could probably squeeze in some of the basics before lunch."

"Sweet," Bethany replied, slipping her sunglasses on again. "Lead the way."

It was all I could do to keep from skipping as I followed them. I was actually hanging with Bethany and Jordan in the same place at the same time. And Daniel was here! We were going on a date that very night! Considering the foul mood I had been in on the bus that morning, I could hardly believe this was the same day. Things were definitely picking up!

"Okay, you all good?" I asked Bethany.

She was kicked back at a table in the hotel's café, her feet up on another chair and her laptop open in front of her. She had a steaming cup of hot coffee and a chocolate éclair, and her iPod was at the ready. Basically the girl was fully in her element.

"Yeah, I just have one question," Bethany said, eyeing my practice uniform. "What are you wearing?"

"You like?" I joked, holding out my light yellow skirt to show the baby blue pleats. "Tara picked them out herself. She wanted us to stand out."

"Mission accomplished."

"We call it the Tweety Bird look," I told her. "Yellow *is* the new black."

"Yeah, you keep telling yourself that," Bethany said, rolling her eyes.

"I gotta go," I said.

"Wouldn't want to be late!" Bethany said. "They might take away your megaphone."

"Har-dee-har," I said. I turned around and headed for the larger restaurant and flashed my light blue briefs at her just to crack her up. It worked.

When I got to the restaurant, the place was already jam-packed with cheerleaders. There was so much perfume and hairspray, a girl could choke. I had a feeling my salad dressing was going to taste like a L'Oréal Vive product. For a second I thought I was never going to find my team in all the mayhem, but they were hard to miss. With all that yellow, our table was glowing like the sun.

I took a deep breath, resolved to tell Tara that I wasn't going to be at dinner that night. I knew she was going to be annoyed, but she was just going to have to deal. A girl has to make certain sacrifices for love.

"Hey, guys!" I said, pulling out a chair next to Mindy. "What's on the menu?"

To save time and money, I supposed, it looked like we had a set lunch. There was a heaping bowl of mixed salad, another of fruit salad and a couple of large platters of sandwiches on the table.

"You're late," Tara said, tearing into a turkey on wheat.

"You guys were early!" I pointed out.

"Whatever, just eat," Tara said grouchily. "One more lateness and I'm making you do laps."

My pulse practically stopped.

"What? You can't—"

"Try me," Tara said, leveling me with a glare. I swear little flames flared up in her pupils.

Wow. I had never seen her look quite that demonesque. Okay, so maybe it wasn't the best time to tell her about tonight. It was probably a better plan to back out at the last minute. Yeah. That's what I would do.

Chicken, a little voice in my head chided. But I had every right to be! The last thing I needed was for Tara to have one of her patented freak-outs in public. Then we'd be labeled as the psycho squad. Judges hear that kind of thing, you know.

"She's just in a bad mood because we have to sit next to the Black Bears at every meal," Whitney whispered, handing me the salad bowl.

I hadn't even noticed on my way in, but now that I looked over my shoulder and saw them, I wondered how I could possibly have missed it. The Black Bears' practice uniforms were jet-black with glittering silver straps and silver around the edging of their skirts. They kind of looked like Darth Vader's personal cheer squad.

"So, what's up with your old squad?" Mindy asked, taking a sip of her water.

"Oh, yeah, I'm sorry about that," I said. "Becca can be a little rash sometimes."

"A little?" Mindy asked.

"Well, that other girl was being seriously rude," I replied. "Becca was just being Becca. I would kill to have the guts to do something like that."

"You're kidding."

"Well, maybe not *that* exactly," I said. "But, you know, at least she stood up for herself."

"Whatever you say," Mindy replied, returning to her lunch.

I wanted to talk about it more, but Mindy clearly didn't. It was kind of frustrating that my old squad and my new squad seemed to want to see the worst in each other. I mean, didn't anyone see that nothing was that black and white? Didn't anyone trust my judgment?

I grabbed a ham and cheese sandwich and gnawed on it while I checked out the rest of the room. It looked like all the high school squads were present, but none of the younger girls, who I guessed had eaten earlier. I couldn't help noticing that not every squad had felt the need to don matching practice uniforms today. Some of them were in shorts and matching tanks. Others looked like they had just been told to wear school colors. I caught a glimpse of the Beavers' table. Everyone there was wearing a red baby T that said BEAVERS in gold lettering across the chest, matched with a pair of black shorts. They looked so cool and comfy. Meanwhile, the short, short hem of my skirt was digging into the back of my thighs like a dull blade.

I also couldn't help noticing—probably because I was counting under my breath—that not all the Beavers were present. Apparently not everyone had this "cheer together, eat together, sleep together" law. Becca and Gia were the most obviously absent. The captain and co-captain. Yeah, things were a little more chill over there.

"Did you see those girls with the feathers in their hair, y'all?" someone at the Black Bears' table said. "Like, we're not in Las Vegas, ladies!"

I glanced across the table at Autumn. Who did these girls think they were, judging people like that? Well, okay, I guess we were all doing it—kind of—but at least we weren't obnoxious enough to do it out *loud*.

"Honestly, I'm kind of disappointed," their captain said with a dramatic sigh. "There just doesn't seem to be any *real* competition this year."

Tara looked like she was one hot sauce–swig away from that cartoon cat explosion.

"I feel bad for some of these teams," another girl said. "They're just so out of their league."

"They may as well just hand over the trophy now," the captain lamented.

"Okay, that's it," Chandra said under her breath, pressing her hands into the table as she stood.

"Sit!" Tara said through her teeth. Chandra dropped down instantly. Tara leaned in over her plate and we all followed suit. "We are not going to stoop to their level, okay? We are above petty posturing. Good sportsmanship is what this weekend is all about. Got it?"

We nodded determinedly and sat up straight again, going about passing the food and pouring drinks. It was all a little false and showy, though, because we weren't paying any attention to each other. Every last one of us had tuned our ears in to what the Black Bears were saying.

"And did you check the uniforms?" another Black Bear said. "Hasn't anyone told these people that retro is so yesterday?"

"I think the chicks at the next table are trying to blind the competition," the captain said, loud enough for everyone to hear. She put her sunglasses on, turned to Tara, and gave her a fluttery little wave. Everyone at the Black Bear table laughed and took out their sunglasses as well.

Tara's teeth were so clenched, I could hear them grinding. She tried to ignore the other squad and reached for the ketchup. Instead she knocked over the saltshaker and the top fell right off, spilling salt everywhere.

"Omigod!" Tara screeched. "Everyone! Throw it over your shoulders! Do it! Throw it over your shoulders!"

Startled, we all did as we were told, which just cracked

the Black Bears up even more. I looked at Mindy, my eyebrows raised. When we got out of this place, Tara was going to have to seek some professional help. Stat.

• • •

"Hey, Trott!" I shouted as we all filed out of the restaurant after lunch. She stopped and waited for me to catch up. "I like your T-shirt."

"Thanks! I don't like your uniform," she replied apologetically.

"A common opinion," I replied. "So, where are Gia and Becca?"

"I don't know," Jordan said with a shrug as we passed into the lobby. "I haven't seen them since the gift shop." She paused. "Oh, God. I hope they didn't get arrested."

"They just went to check out the beach," Maria Rinaldi said with a laugh, overhearing.

"So you guys don't all have to eat together all the time?" I asked.

Jordan knit her brows. "What are you, kidding? We have to spend enough time together this weekend," she said jokingly.

"Good point."

Sigh. If I were still on the Beavers, I wouldn't have to feel guilty—or scared to even bring up—skipping a meal to go out with Daniel. There would be no laps for lateness or talk of hair dye. Of course, if I were still with the Beavers, that would mean I'd still live in Jersey and I never would have even *met* Daniel.

Life!

• • •

118

When I first walked into the ballroom where we were going to be practicing, I thought I was going to freeze to death. The air-conditioning was jacked up to a level that would have made my father proud. Goose bumps popped up all over my arms and legs and any little hairs I'd missed around my knees stood on end. But now that we were running through our routine for the third time, I understood why the powers-that-be kept it so cold. The collar of my Suzie Sunshine uniform was already wet with sweat.

"All you fans, yell 'Go!'"

"Go!"

Chandra and Autumn pushed me up into my double base extension and I thrust the blue-and-yellow GO sign over my head, making sure to nod and smile as I shouted and pinched a penny with my butt cheeks. Man, there was a lot to remember sometimes.

Steven snapped a few pictures of us as, across the practice area, Jordan, Becca, Gia and the rest of the Beavers stopped what they were doing and lined up to observe. I saw Becca whisper something to Gia as they watched our routine with hawklike eyes. Today was all about sizing up the competition. The Black Bears and the squad from Tennessee hadn't arrived yet, but I was sure that if they were there, they would be doing the same thing.

As for me, I was just psyched to have the chance to show my old team what my new team could do.

"All you fans, yell 'Crabs!'"

"Crabs!"

Across from me, Kimberly held up the CRABS sign.

"Go!"

"Crabs!"

"Go!"

"Crabs!"

"One more time!" Tara shouted.

"Go!"

"Crabs!"

The music started up again, and I tossed the sign down and cradled out of the stunt. As we whipped back into our dancing frenzy, the Beavers watched us, and I couldn't help but notice that several of them looked impressed. I caught Jordan's eye and grinned. She winked and grinned right back.

I popped up into my last, highest throw and executed my twist in the air. I tried not to close my eyes as I went upside down, but it's a little freaky watching the world overturn itself. Still, I knew my teammates would be there to catch me. They hadn't dropped me once.

Well, not since the first time we tried this one, anyway.

As soon as we hit our final poses, the Beavers erupted into applause and appreciative hollers. I glanced at Mindy and shrugged one shoulder. See? My old squad isn't all bad. They know a good performance when they see it.

"All right, ladies! Looking good!" Coach Holmes cheered as we gathered around her. True to her unity beliefs, she was wearing a bright yellow sweatshirt over light blue leggings. Somehow she didn't even look pained about it. "I just got a call from Tara's mom, and the parental caravan should be arriving any minute. Why don't you guys take a break and go out to meet your parents? Good work!"

"All right, everyone! Hands in!" Tara said. We all gathered in a huddle and placed our hands in the middle. Everyone was winded and rosy. Steven climbed up on a chair and took a couple of shots of our hands from above. Very artistic! "Crabs on three," Tara said. "One! Two! Three!"

"Crabs!"

We all clapped as we broke off, grabbing water bottles and towels from our bags. I placed my foot on a chair and was leaning down to retie my sneaker and catch my breath when Tara plopped onto one of the folding chairs next to me.

"So, Gobrowski, if we're going to do your hair, we should probably do it now," she said.

I dropped my foot to the floor. "Tara—"

"I'm serious, Annisa. Semifinals are tomorrow morning," Tara said, dabbing her neck with her towel. "It's now or never."

"Mmmm, how about never?" I replied.

Chandra joined us and stood next to me, her arms folded over her chest. "Are we *still* talking about this hair-dye thing? God, Tara, why don't you just leave her alone?"

Both Erin and Jaimee looked up and glanced at each other. They moseyed over as well, as if they sensed another chance to campaign. A few of the other cheerleaders took extra time organizing their things and stretching out, pretending they weren't sticking around just to hear what happened. Sage blatantly stood there behind Tara, not caring what I thought, apparently.

"No one asked for your opinion, Chandra," Tara snapped.

"Actually, I kind of *like* what she has to say," I said.

"There's a stunner," Erin put in.

"What, you think I should do it too?" I asked, surprised.

"Well, if it's for the good of the team . . . ," she said, lifting her shoulders.

Unreal. I had always thought Erin was cool, but now it was like she agreed with anything and everything Tara said.

"What if we compromise?" Jaimee suggested, clasping her hands. "What about temporary dye? Or maybe just some highlights?"

"*Et tu*, Jaimee?" I said, arching my eyebrows.

"What are you afraid of, Annisa? Think Daniel will dump you if you go blonde? Afraid you won't be different enough for him anymore?" Sage asked.

My toes actually curled as I glared at her. Why the heck did she always have to bring up Daniel? And what did she mean, "different enough"? Had he told her that he liked me *because* I was different? Did they discuss me behind my back on their secret phone calls?

But he said *he didn't call her,* my shoulder angel reminded me.

He could have lied, duh, the devil piped in.

"Low blow, Barnard," Chandra said, defending me. Sage just rolled her eyes.

"I don't understand why you're being so unreasonable about this," Tara snapped. "We're talking about nationals here."

"And I don't understand why you think our winning nationals depends on the color of my hair," I replied. "Look at the Beavers!" I said, throwing out my hand. My old squad was practicing a pyramid on the other side of the room. "They're brunette, redheaded, blonde. White, black, Latina. God, what do you think the captain of the Black Bears would say if someone told her to dye that gorgeous hair of hers?"

"Oh, so now you're not only rooting for your old squad,

122

but you're a Black Bears fan as well?" Tara asked, standing. "Whose side are you on, anyway?"

My jaw dropped. Tara was going straight-up insane.

"Look, we have until tonight," Tara said, draping her towel over her shoulders. "Just think about it. I know you'll do the right thing."

She turned and walked off, followed by Sage and a few others. I was too speechless to stop her. She really thought she was going to guilt me into this, didn't she? Did the girl not know me at all?

"She will!" Erin shouted after her. "She'll think about it!"

I gaped at Erin. This captainship thing was making everyone go bonkers. I half wanted to check the back of Erin's head for her other face.

"What?" she asked. "I just said you'd *think* about it."

"Maybe you *should* think about it, Annisa," Jaimee said. "Unless you don't want to."

Erin scoffed and rolled her eyes.

"Come on," Chandra said, hooking her arm around my neck. "Let's go find our parents."

I grabbed my water bottle and let her lead me away from the others. At this point, I was practically salivating to see my family. They may be nuts in their own ways, but at this point they were pretty much the sanest people in my life.

Scary.

Phoebe pushed herself away from the wall where she had been leaning as soon as Chandra and I stepped out of the ballroom. She glanced over her shoulder to make sure Tara wasn't anywhere around.

"So, she's still on your case, huh?" she asked.

"Like an ambulance-chasing lawyer," Chandra said.

I snorted a laugh. "What do you think, Phoebe?"

"Well, I guess I kind of see both sides of it," Phoebe said as we headed for the lobby. "I can tell you one thing, though. She's never going to let it go."

"Even I could've told you that," Chandra said.

We stepped into the airy center of the hotel, which was once again filled with people milling around, shouting and squealing. With the stories-high ceiling and the huge dome skylight, the place had the perfect acoustics to make an already loud group sound even louder.

"Can't you just think of it as a team-unity thing?" Phoebe suggested, tightening her own dark blonde ponytail. "Like those hockey player guys who all grow beards during the play-offs?"

"They do?" I asked.

"Totally," Phoebe replied. "As long as they keep winning, no one shaves, no matter how grizzly they look."

"Huh. Never would have pegged you for a hockey fan," I said.

"I'm a very deep and complex person," Phoebe replied indignantly.

"Deep and complex people do not have pink walls and lace duvet covers," I deadpanned. "Actually, neither do hockey fans." Phoebe hip-checked me into Chandra and we laughed. "Okay! I take it back!"

"Well, at least Tara's not asking you to grow a beard," Chandra put in.

"You're not changing your mind now too, are you?" I asked her.

"Me? Change my mind? Have you not met me?" Chandra asked. "Stubborn is my middle name. I'm with you, kid."

"Thanks," I replied. "Besides, *every* guy on a hockey team grows a beard for unity, right?"

Phoebe nodded.

"Then why am I the only one who has to dye her hair?" I asked, raising my eyebrows.

Phoebe and Chandra exchanged a look. "You should definitely go to law school," Phoebe said.

"Oh, there are my brothers!" Chandra exclaimed, pointing at a pair of guys who looked just like her, but with shorter, darker hair. "Losers!" she shouted gleefully, running over to them and jumping into the arms of the taller one.

Steven, who was circling the lobby snapping pics of my teammates with their families, caught their reunion on his memory card.

"I thought she had four brothers," I said to Phoebe.

"One lives in Santa Barbara and the other is always world-traveling," Phoebe said.

"Right! The photographer," I said, remembering.

"Lucky bastard," Phoebe said under her breath. "Right now I'd like to be pretty much anywhere but here."

I blinked, intrigued. "Why? What's going on?"

"Hey, girls!" Autumn said, joining us.

"Autumn, hey! How's my favorite earth goddess?" Phoebe asked boisterously. Clearly she was avoiding my question, but I didn't give up that easily.

"Phoebe, if you need to talk about anything, you—"

"Hey! There's your parents," Phoebe said, nudging my arm. "And . . . is that . . . Gabe?"

We all turned to look. Sure enough, there were my mom and dad checking in at the front desk. Mom was wearing a black pantsuit with her red hair pulled back in a low pony-tail, her makeup perfectly applied. Dad was looking frumpy as usual in a plaid shirt and wrinkly chinos. Next to them was a person I could only assume was my brother, although I had never seen his red hair that short or carefully coiffed in my life.

"I thought he was a surf bum," Autumn said, confused. "What happened to the baggy shorts and the Tevas? I liked the baggy shorts and the Tevas."

"I have no idea," I said.

Gabe had topped a pair of trendy sneakers with flat-front chinos and a toggle belt. His white T-shirt bore not a wrinkle nor a stain and over that he was wearing a pristine light-weight brown suede jacket. He pulled off his aviator sunglasses to check out a couple of girls who walked by and they both grinned and giggled in response.

"Ladies," I heard Gabe say with a smirk.

"Oh, God. He's gone metrosexual on us," I said, rolling my eyes. "Excuse me. Mom! Dad!"

I jogged across the lobby, pleats flying, and gave my mother and father both a big sweaty hug.

"Annisa! You look so sweet!" my mother said, stepping back to check out my ensemble. "Very retro."

"Thanks," I said.

My mom is a personal shopper and she is always taking note of people's fashion statements. Too bad the Black Bears and their snarky captain weren't around to hear her comments. I turned to Gabe and clucked my tongue, looking him up and down.

"Nice look, Gabe. Finally discover the Bravo network?"

Gabe is Mr. Chameleon. He changes not only his look, but his entire life philosophy about once every three months. Of course, I never thought I'd see him embracing the *GQ* lifestyle. He's always been a little too chill to worry about such things as, oh, grooming and bathing.

Gabe put out his arms and executed a little spin. "I thought it was about time for me to mature my style a tad," he said with a cocky little twist of the lips. "You feeling it?"

Clearly he had also ditched the "dudes" and "whoas" of his former persona.

"I'm feeling *something*," I said, putting a hand to my stomach.

"Oh, Annisa!" my mother scolded. "I think he looks adorable." She grabbed my brother's chin between her fingers and gave him a good squeeze, puckering his face. Then she hit him with a big smacking kiss on the cheek. "My Gabe is all grown up!"

I laughed as Gabe squirmed. "Mom! Please! I'm a man over here!"

Suddenly, Steven was upon us with his camera. "May I?" he asked, looking at my dad.

"Since when do you ask permission?" I joked.

Steven blushed and shrugged. Apparently he was a parental kiss-butt.

"Annisa, don't be rude," my mother said.

"I wasn't!" I replied.

"Steven! Nice to see you again!" my father added. He had finished up at the front desk and was now folding his wallet into his pocket. "Of course you can have a picture."

He pulled us all together with his great wingspan and we all smiled for Steven's camera. Everyone except Gabe, who struck a pout worthy of *Details* magazine.

"Thanks!" Steven said, then hustled off.

"So, back to this man thing," my father said, turning to Gabe. "Will you be paying for your own room then, man that you are?"

Gabe paled slightly. Wait a second, was he wearing *mascara?*

"Uh . . . I haven't exactly gotten my last work-study check, actually, Dad."

I leaned forward, squinting at his eyelashes, and he quickly covered his eyes with his sunglasses. "Can we go check out the pool?"

"Good idea," my mom said, slipping her arm through his.

"I hope that stuff is waterproof!" I shouted after them.

My father laughed and shook his head. "Are you girls having fun?"

"It's been great, Dad," I said, putting aside anything negative that had happened so far. My father really didn't need to know that my friends were trying to pressure me in to dyeing my hair. He might actually kidnap me and take me home if he heard that. For a guy who moves all over the country for his job, he's not big on change. "And guess what? Jordan is here with the Beavers! They're competing too!"

"Jordan? That's a nice surprise!" my father said. "Although I might have trouble deciding which team to support."

"You're hysterical, really," I said.

"I try," my father replied. "Hey, isn't that your friend Bethany?"

I looked up and grinned. Bethany was trotting along with a group of the ESPN crew guys, her digital video camera poised as she peppered them with questions. One of the guys laughed, flashing an incredible smile, and Bethany actually blushed. I didn't even think that was possible.

I guess everyone was finding something to enjoy on this trip.

• • •

"Phoebe! What's going on with you?" Coach asked as we all hit the mats after another run-through. "You had that section down earlier."

"Sorry, Coach," Phoebe said, reaching for her towel. Some of the hair had fallen from her ponytail and was plastered to her neck and face. "I'll get it back."

"All right. Make sure you do," Coach said.

I glanced at Mindy. "What's up with her?" I whispered.

"She's looked like a zombie ever since break," Mindy replied with a shrug. She stretched her leg out and leaned over to touch her toes. Phoebe covered her face with the towel and held it there for longer than was absolutely necessary. Something was definitely up with her. She was acting just like she had when I first joined the squad, back when her parents had separated.

"Maybe you should find yourself a good-luck charm," Tara suggested. "Get your head back in the game."

I wanted to smack the back of her head. Phoebe was supposed to be one of her best friends. How about saying something *constructive?*

"Yeah, thanks, Tara. I'll get right on that," Phoebe said sarcastically.

I resolved right then and there to talk to Phoebe when we were dismissed, whether she wanted to talk to me or not. Clearly she needed to get *something* off her chest.

"Well, all right, girls. I think that's enough for today," Coach Holmes said finally. "Let's get stretched out."

Tara got up to lead us through stretching. Feeling my heart rate slow to normal and my muscles quiver with pleasure as I stretched was perfection. Of course, it would have been a lot better if not for the presence of the Black Bears.

They had already started practice when we got back from our parental break and they hadn't so much as paused since. They were like soldiers over there, shouting and tumbling and doing their jumps in perfect unison. It was clear that every other squad in the room was intimidated.

As I bent over for a calf stretch, the Black Bears' captain went flying into the air, executing a perfect layout. It looked effortless. When she came down into her partners' arms, she flew right back up into a liberty.

Whitney whistled, impressed. I saw a bunch of my teammates exchange wide-eyed glances.

"Don't look at them! Look at me!" Tara ordered.

Everyone snapped back to attention. Still, we could see

what was going on over there out of the corners of our eyes and it was far too pretty. By the time we were done stretching, we all wanted out of there.

"Nice work, girls! See you at dinner!" Coach Holmes called out.

Or some of us, I added silently, my stomach flopping. I still hadn't told anyone I had decided to ditch for Daniel. Maybe it was about time I tried to talk to Tara.

"Hey."

I glanced up to find Phoebe hovering over me, looking pale.

"Hey," I replied. "You okay?"

"Not exactly," Phoebe said, glancing over her shoulder. "Do you want to get some ice cream or something?"

"Sure," I said, quickly gathering my things. It was clear that Phoebe wanted to talk. Before regionals she had confided in me about the problems her parents were having, and I knew that most of the squad wasn't in on as many details as I was. If Phoebe wanted to borrow my ear above anyone else's, it was probably about her family. I just hoped the news wasn't *too* bad.

"Let's go," I said. We hoisted our bags onto our shoulders and headed for the door.

"Hey! Annisa!"

Becca jogged over to us and Phoebe looked at the floor. My pulse actually raced over the fact that Becca was talking to me. This was going to take some getting used to.

"What's up?" I asked.

"Do you think I could . . . uh . . . talk to you for a sec?" she asked, eyeing Phoebe.

"Um . . . actually . . ."

"Just for a second, I swear," Becca pleaded, lacing her fingers together.

I glanced at Phoebe hopefully. I mean, this was Becca Richardson begging to talk to *me*. What was I supposed to do, turn her down?

"Just for a second?" I said to Phoebe. "Then I'll catch up with you in the café?"

"Sure. Whatever," she said flatly.

She turned and jogged off before I could say another word. Was it my imagination, or did she seem like she was on the verge of tears? I stepped to the door and glanced down the hall in time to see her catch up to Tara.

Okay. No harm, no foul. She had her best friend to talk to, after all. And meanwhile, Becca Richardson was hovering.

"Okay. I'm all yours," I told Becca, trying to ignore the hollowness in my chest that Phoebe's departure had left behind.

"Would you mind watching us do a run-through?" Becca asked as the rest of the Beavers caught their breath on the mat, watching us with interest. "We could use a few pointers."

I almost pinched myself. Becca Richardson was asking *me* for advice? *The* Becca Richardson?

"Oh! Uh, sure. Absolutely," I said, trying not to be too giddy.

"Fab! Thank you *so* much. Everyone! Annisa's going to critique us!" Becca shouted, jogging over to the squad. "Let's show her what we can do!"

A few of the Beavers cheered as they got into formation. I stood at the edge of the mat and placed my bag on the floor, rolling my tired shoulders back. Coach Martinez started the music, then walked over to join me.

"Your squad looks great, Gobrowski," she said.

"Thanks, Coach. I miss you guys, though."

She smiled. "We miss you too."

The Beavers started their routine with a domino-style stunt line, one heel stretch going up at a time and to the beat. Already I couldn't believe how far they had come. The last time we had tried a basket toss, Jordan had flown halfway across the room and the bases had to run to catch her. We didn't attempt much after that. But these stunts were perfect.

"Wow, nice," I said as they started their first dance sequence.

"They've been working really hard," Coach told me.

"Obviously," I said with a grin.

Gia was in the front of the formation now, grooving with everything she had. She had always been an amazing dancer—one of the best in the school—but she didn't look quite right up front. Then I realized it was her face. She looked kind of bored and distracted. The judges were not going to like that.

Donnie Walker, the girl who had replaced me, hit a huge tumbling run and raced back to the formation to be thrown. Her energy was great, as were Jordan's and Maria's and Becca's, but everyone else looked as apathetic as they always had.

"Everyone, stand up and shout 'Beavers!'" the team chanted.

"Beavers!" Coach and I yelled.

"Everyone stand up and shout 'Go, red-and-gold!'"

"Go, red-and-gold!"

They held up colorful, glittery signs that I could tell Jordan had made herself. She was definitely the artistic one on the squad. A queasy sort of uncomfortable warmth overcame me as I imagined her alone in her room working on them. I wished I had been there with her. It was so bizarre to think of her going about our old lives without me. And the team had obviously been fine since I left. Not that I expected them to crumble without me, but I guess I never thought they might improve. Especially to this level.

They launched into their final dance sequence and ended up in a dazzling pyramid. Everyone hit their places on the beat and they were all grinning at the end—even Gia. The music stopped and Coach and I cheered loudly. The Tennessee team applauded as well and Jordan beamed as they came down from their stunts. The Black Bears, of course, were completely focused on themselves.

"So? What do you think?" Becca asked, walking over to me with her hands on her hips.

The entire squad gathered around to listen to what I had to say. Gulp. My heart was suddenly in my throat. Did I tell the truth and risk the wrath of Gia and the others, or did I just say they were perfect and hightail it out of there?

"Come on, Goober. Dish it," Gia said.

"Yeah," a few others chorused.

"Uh . . . okay," I said finally. "Well, it was really awesome. The stunts were amazing," I said, earning a few appreciative grins. "But there was a little sloppiness on the dance sequences. A couple of you were off tempo," I said. "And a few people need to work on their expressions, you know?"

The grins were rapidly fading. Gulp gulp.

"Like who?" Gia demanded.

"Like . . . you know . . . a few people," I said, my throat going dry.

"Gia, you know you're one of them," Coach Martinez said. "We've talked about this a hundred times."

"Coach, I'm not gonna bug my eyes out of my head," Gia said.

"You don't have to!" I told her. "Just . . . try smiling."

A few of her teammates snickered as Gia scowled.

"Oh, and you could work on your high V's," I added finally. "Everyone seemed to be at a different level. Mostly they need to be higher. Like this."

I put my arms up in a V. This was one of the first things Tara and Coach Holmes had drilled into my head when I first made the Sand Dune squad. I glanced at Jordan. Her mouth was set in a tight line and she instantly looked down at her feet. She jammed her toe into the floor a few times, pointedly ignoring me. I felt my spirits droop and put my arms down. What was that about?

"All right! You heard what she said, people! Let's get our butts in gear!" Becca shouted, shooing them back onto the mat.

"Thanks for your help," Coach Martinez told me, patting me on the back.

"No problem," I said.

Jordan turned around without a second glance, and when Coach started the music again, she was staring straight off at a fixed point somewhere above my head. I tried to catch her eye, but she refused to look at me. I could *see* her concentrating to keep from looking my way. Was she mad at me? Why? She had heard Becca ask for my help, hadn't she? It wasn't as if I'd gone over there and critiqued them for *fun*. Feeling hollow, I picked up my bag and slunk out of there.

Jordan had never been mad at me before. Not once in the last four years. And I couldn't even pull her aside and ask her what was wrong. She was in there with her squad and I was out here alone. Even though we had been living a thousand miles away from each other for the last few months, I had never felt so separated from her and I didn't like the gaping hole that had opened in my heart. Not at all.

That night I got a little taste of what college might be like. Not the classes or the campus, but the getting ready in one tiny room with female roommates. Tara was off meeting with Coach Holmes before dinner, but Whitney had joined us, claiming that Chandra, Autumn and Felice were taking up too much space in their room. Now, instead, she was encroaching on our meager mirror—and with Mindy, Phoebe, Whitney and I all dressing and doing our hair at the same time, it was total chaos. Between the curling iron, the hair dryer and the flurry of clothes and shoes, it was like backstage at NYC Fashion Week. Only far less fabulous.

"Oops! Sorry!" Mindy said as she spritzed perfume right in my eye.

I gasped, inhaling a cloud of perfume. The ensuing coughing fit threw me back a few blind steps and I stumbled over Phoebe's pink leather sandals.

"Oof!" she said as I crushed her foot under mine.

"Sorry!" I cried. I waved a hand in front of my face to clear the smog of products. "I think I need to take a breather," I told them, blinking rapidly and smacking my tongue against the roof of my mouth in an attempt to lose the sour perfume taste. I staggered away from the mirror and toward the bed, where I sat and took a nice, long breath.

"You okay?" Whitney asked, fluffing her hair as she followed after me. She leaned in toward the mirror over the dresser and blinked her eyes a few times, checking her makeup.

"Fine," I lied.

Time to get a grip. I was a klutz on a good day, but when the butterflies in my stomach started doing double backflips, it totally threw me off balance. First of all, I was nervous about my date with Daniel. This could finally be the night he asked me to be his girlfriend. If so, I wanted everything to go perfectly, and those are usually the times that *nothing* goes perfectly. So, yeah, there was that overwhelming über-fear. But I was even more nervous about bailing out on dinner with the squad. What if they flipped out on me?

Yeah. Some "what if." The question was actually how big the flip-out would be.

I smoothed the skirt of my dark blue and white Hawaiian print mini dress and glanced at the phone, willing it to ring. I had left Jordan a message over an hour ago and she had yet to call me back. Something was definitely going on with her and I wanted to talk to her about it. But I also needed her advice and a serious pep talk about tonight. After all, she was the one who had convinced me that the Daniel date was a good idea. Why wasn't she calling me back?

Okay, all you have to do is tell Whitney or Mindy what's going on, I told myself, taking another deep breath. *They're your friends. They'll make an excuse for you.* I was sure that at least these two would understand.

I stood up again just as Phoebe emerged from the "primping area." She looked cute and casual in a light pink top, khaki shorts and strappy pink sandals. I still hadn't had a chance to talk to her about whatever had been bothering her that afternoon, but she seemed to be feeling better, so I assumed that chatting with Tara had done the trick. Either way, I didn't want to bring it up with Mindy and Whitney around, just in case she wanted to talk alone.

"So, Annisa, what's up with the dress?" Whitney asked. She finished inspecting her face and grabbed her bag. "I mean, you look hot. Too hot for dinner with the squad."

Nice! A perfect opening!

"You're not ditching to have dinner with your parents, are you?" Phoebe put in. "'Cause you're really supposed to have meals with the squad."

Huh. Maybe this was going to be harder than I thought.

"Actually, I—"

There was a knock at the door and I flinched. Could Daniel be here already? But when I opened the door, it wasn't my crush that was standing there looking nervous enough to faint. It was Bethany.

"I need to talk to you," she said, grabbing my arm and yanking me into the hall.

"Okay, *ow,*" I said, rubbing my shoulder. "I might need that tomorrow."

"Cry me a river. I got real problems," Bethany said shortly. She was shifting her weight from leg to leg like she had to pee. I had never seen her look so kinetic.

"What's going on?" I asked.

Bethany looked over her shoulder, glanced at the still-closed door and leaned toward me to whisper, "I think I got a date."

"What?" I squealed.

"Shhh!" she said, widening her eyes in a menacing way.

"Bethany! That's great!" I whispered. "Who is he? Where'd you meet him? What's he like?" The look on her face was so blank that for a second the ground tilted beneath me. Suddenly I realized that I had never heard Bethany even *talk* about boys or crushes before. "Or . . . she?" I said, my throat dry with embarrassment. "Sorry, is it a she?"

"No! It's a *he*," she replied. "Not that I wouldn't *kill* to see the look on my parents' faces if I came home with a girl, but unfortunately, I'm hetero."

"Okay, so what's he like?" I asked.

"Gorgeous," she said, groaning like *gorgeous* was a horrifying skin disease. She leaned back against the wall and whacked her head against it. "Too gorgeous. He might be the devil, actually. Only the devil could be that good-looking."

"Wow. You've got it bad," I said, grinning.

"That's why you have to come with me," she said, her eyes pleading. Bethany. Pleading. Who knew it was possible?

"Come with you? When?"

"Tonight. Now," she said. "Did I not mention that?"

My heart twisted inside my chest. "Bethany! Come on! Not now! I can't. I'm going out with Daniel," I whispered.

She leveled me with a stare. "I believe it's called a double date. At least I *think* that's what I've heard."

"But tonight might be the night he . . . you know," I said through my teeth.

Bethany narrowed her eyes and stood up defiantly. "Annisa Louise Gobrowski—"

"My middle name is not Louise."

"So what? You need to remember that your Mr. Perfectly Boring wouldn't even *be* here if it wasn't for me," she said. "I cannot do this alone."

"Why not?" I asked, throwing my hands up.

"Because!" she replied. She looked at the floor and screwed her mouth up to the side. "Because this is my *first date*," she said quietly. "I *need* backup or I *will* screw this up."

I blinked. That may have been the most blatantly self-doubting thing I had ever heard Bethany say.

"Come on, Annisa, you owe me."

I looked into her brown eyes and felt myself cave. It wasn't often that Bethany looked vulnerable, so when she did, I'll admit it, I was moved. Besides, I did not want to be the subject of another sucks-to-be-us.com editorial, thank you very much. *The Devil Wears Pleats,* which she had written after I had ditched her to participate in the prank war, did not do much for my ego.

"All right, fine," I said finally. "Double date it is."

"Yes," Bethany said. "You won't regret it."

"What's this guy's name, anyway?" I asked.

"Chuck," she said.

"*Chuck?*"

"Chuck," she replied. "Got a problem?"

"No. Of course not," I replied.

But I would in a second. I still had to break the news of my date—my *double* date—to the squad. I knocked on the door and Whitney instantly whipped it open.

"You don't really think we're going to let you skip dinner, do you?" she said.

My heart dropped. "What do you have, bionic hearing?"

Mindy and Phoebe were hanging back by the primping area, looking concerned. Clearly Whitney had shared everything she had overheard with them. Yippee.

Whitney looked at Bethany. "Can you excuse us for a second?"

"Sure," Bethany said. But she walked inside anyway.

Whitney sighed in an exasperated way and was about to close the door to give me my proverbial lumps when Daniel appeared in the doorway.

"Hey," Daniel said with that mind-blowing smile. He was wearing a soft-looking gray V-neck sweater and jeans. Yum.

"Hey," I replied.

"You ready to—"

"Annisa? We really need to talk," Whitney said.

She didn't give me much time to answer. Instead she tugged me away from the door by my wrist and the heavy thing almost slammed in Daniel's face. He caught it just in time and came in. I saw him greeting Bethany as I was basically tossed into the primping area.

"What do you think you're doing?" Phoebe asked me under her breath. "You cannot miss dinner with the squad to go out with Daniel and Bethany and some dude named Chuck."

Wow. Whitney got every detail.

"What's the big deal?" I asked.

"The big deal is, Tara will kill you and serve you up for breakfast," Whitney said.

"Annisa, come on," Mindy said calmly. "We're here for nationals. You have to make the squad your number-one priority right now."

"But it's just dinner," I told them. "One meal."

"God, Annisa! It's three days away from your boyfriend," Phoebe hissed. "Can't you put the brakes on your love life for three damn days?"

Was she kidding? Whose love life was she talking about? Because mine never seemed to get out of the slow lane. "How am I supposed to put the brakes on my love life when I haven't even hit the gas?" I whispered.

They glanced at one another and Mindy shrugged. Phoebe rolled her eyes and Whitney looked away. It was like they just didn't know what to do with me. Well, neither did I at this point. I mean, I did see their side. I did. It *was* only three days and unity was important to the squad. Logically, it made sense.

But try telling that to my heart. All my heart wanted was to be with Daniel. To give him a chance to finally come through. To go to bed tonight knowing I was his girlfriend. What if I went out there and blew him off and he kicked me to the curb? Or worse, what if he went back to Sage? Did I really want to ruin my potential first relationship for one meal with the squad? If I were sick, I wouldn't have to go down there and no one would think the worse of me, right? Well, I *was* sick. Heartsick. How's that for an excuse?

I took a deep breath and looked at Whitney. She was staring me down, just waiting for me to do the right thing. My conscience wanted to side with her. After all, I was used to toeing the line, being the good girl, doing as I was told. It went against my very nature to do otherwise.

He'll understand, the angel on my shoulder said. *If there's anyone who knows about following the rules, it's Daniel.*

Except for the fact that he had broken a few big fat ones when he had skipped school to come down here. For me.

Still, I was about give in to second nature and tell my teammates I would get rid of Daniel and Bethany (how, I had no idea), when my eyes fell on the box of Herbal Essences hair dye that was still sitting on the counter. Only now the kit had been opened and all the little pieces—the bottles and plastic gloves and instructions—had been laid out in a row. Like it was ready to go. Like it was a foregone conclusion that when we got back from dinner, we were dyeing my hair. Up until now, Phoebe's shower towel had been balled up on top of it, hiding it. But now I realized Tara must have prepped it before she left for her meeting.

I could just imagine her smug face as she unpacked the box. My fingers clenched into angry fists. Tara Timothy was not the boss of me!

"You know what, you guys? This is my life," I snapped, grabbing my purse. "I'm sick of everyone on this squad telling me what to do and who to talk to and how to do my hair."

Becca and Gia and Jordan would never stand for this. They would never stick around and be treated this way.

"Annisa," Mindy said. "You know we just—"

"Care about the team," I finished for her. "Too bad that's all you seem to care about."

"You know that's not true," Whitney said.

I swallowed hard. I didn't want to be mad at Mindy and Whitney. They were my best friends on the squad. But right then it felt as if they had aligned themselves with the enemy.

"Tara is going to burst a blood vessel when you don't show," Phoebe told me. "What are we supposed to tell her?"

"Tell her whatever you want. Tell her I'm out with Daniel. Tell all of them for all I care," I said. "And while you're at it, you can tell them what they can do with their box of hair dye."

I turned around, grabbed Daniel's hand and whisked him out into the hallway. Bethany followed gleefully and let the door slam behind her. Suddenly I felt free and strong and like myself again. If I wasn't going to stand up for me, no one would.

"Everything okay?" Daniel asked.

"Yeah, it's fine," I told him. *It's just one meal,* I told myself. *One little meal.*

"Is it true? Is Tara Timothy really going to have an aneurysm when you don't show?" Bethany asked.

I felt a pang of guilt and fear as the elevator doors slid open in front of us. "Probably."

Bethany rubbed her hands together as she stepped into the elevator. "This day just keeps getting better."

"Honestly, I don't think I've ever been this mad!" I said, my foot bouncing up and down under the tablecloth. We were sitting at an outdoor table at a tiny restaurant overlooking the crashing surf. There were white twinkle lights, a jazz band playing on a small stage, and a light breeze making the flames on the votive candles dance. It probably would have been very romantic if I hadn't been going berserk. "I thought they were my friends! What kind of friends tell you who to hang out with and what to do and when to dye your hair?"

"Friendship is a boat that holds two in fair weather, one in foul," Chuck said, his deep voice reverberating over the table.

"Exactly!" I agreed, throwing my hand up.

I wasn't actually all that sure what he had said, but everything out of his mouth sounded wise. Chuck was a broad-shouldered, light-skinned African American guy of very few words. He had these piercing green eyes and he looked right through you whenever you spoke, like he was not only taking in every word, but analyzing them to the last syllable. Bethany couldn't take her eyes off of him.

"That's kind of cynical, isn't it?" Daniel asked, looking uncertain.

"That's why I like him," Bethany said. If she got any closer, she was going to be resting her chin on his shoulder.

"Can I take your drink order?" the waitress asked, appearing at the edge of the table.

"I'd like a Coke, please," I said.

"Annisa, are you sure caffeine is the way to go right now?" Daniel asked, looking at my jittering leg.

I actually glared at him. He raised his hands in defeat. "Get the lady a Coke!" he said. "I'll stick with water, thanks."

As Bethany and Chuck placed their orders, I felt Daniel's hand cover mine under the table, on top of my thigh. His skin was so warm, and his touch sent a pleasant tingle all through my body. I smiled and my leg calmed down considerably. He squeezed my fingers and I squeezed back.

"Everything's going to be okay," he said.

I wanted to believe him. I did. But it didn't feel that way. And besides, wasn't this the person whose phone number was on Sage Barnard's caller ID? Why should I trust him?

Look, Annisa. You either believe him or you don't, my shoulder angel said. *Which is it gonna be?*

I let out a breath, expelling as much negativity as possible along with it. For now, I had to believe him. If I didn't, then I was out to dinner with a liar, and did I really want a liar asking me to be his girlfriend?

Could I possibly have been more confused?

"I'm sorry," I said finally, adding a self-deprecating smile. "I'll calm down now."

"It's okay. You're upset," Daniel said. "For the record, I like your hair the way it is."

I beamed. Okay. He got points for that one.

"There's no truer beauty than that which God gave us," Chuck said.

Bethany reached up and self-consciously touched her own hair, which had been purple not all that long ago. I wasn't even sure if that jet-black she was sporting was even close to her natural brown.

"Thanks," I told him. "So, this place is amazing, huh?" I said, taking in my surroundings for real. "How did you find it?"

"I did some research in the hotel lobby," Daniel said. "The concierge guy recommended it. He said his sister waitresses here."

"Cool," I said, trying to relax my shoulders. I picked up the menu and glanced over the options. It was time for me to forget the squad drama. I could deal with them later. I was here now. With Daniel. I had to concentrate on putting my Sage-related fears aside and focus on him and our date.

"So, Chuck, you work for ESPN?" Daniel asked.

"For now," Chuck said. "I'm saving money for this spring."

"What's this spring?" Bethany asked.

"I'm going on an art tour of Europe," Chuck told her.

"What do you do on an art tour?" Daniel asked.

"See all the greats," Chuck replied, taking a sip of his water. "I start art school in the fall."

I thought Bethany was going to swoon. "You're an artist?"

"I'm trying to be," he said with a small smile.

"What's your medium?"

"Metal, mostly. Modern sculpture," he replied. "Though I've done a little inking as well."

"Oh, God. Like, comic book inking?" she asked.

"My friend and I have our own book," he replied. *"Downer Boy."*

"You have your own *book*?" Bethany practically fell off her chair.

"I think it's true love," Daniel whispered to me.

"Yeah, if there is such a thing," I muttered. I guess I was feeling a little cynical myself.

Daniel looked at me for a moment. "Are you okay?"

"Yeah. Fine," I said. Actually, I was getting kind of antsy. Call me crazy, but as happy as I was that Bethany seemed to be smitten, it wasn't easy watching it happen while I was wondering what was going on in my maybe-boyfriend's head.

Daniel looked around, as if at a loss. On the small dance floor a couple of people were swaying to the music. "Do you maybe . . . want to dance?"

"Sounds like a plan," I replied, pushing myself up. Anything was better than sitting still.

Daniel held on to my hand as we walked over to the dance floor and my heart melted a bit. He didn't seem to want to let go of me. Would a guy who still wanted to be with his ex behave this way? Doubtful.

"So, you want me to take Tara Timothy down later? Because I will," Daniel said, placing his arms around my waist.

"Let's not talk about the squad anymore," I said.

"Fine by me," Daniel replied with a tentative smile.

He held me a little closer and we started to step back and forth, turning in a tiny circle on the dance floor.

"So, is everything okay, Annisa?" he asked, sounding strained. "I mean, not with the squad. With us."

A cold fist of ice closed around my heart. Was he going to tell me about Sage now? Was this his way of broaching the subject?

"Why do you ask?" I said, trying to remain as calm as possible.

"Because, well . . . there's something I want to say, but it's gonna sound stupid," Daniel told me, his voice low. "But if you're mad at me or something . . ."

"I'm not mad at you," I said, holding my breath. Whatever this was, I wanted to get it over with. "Just tell me."

"It's just . . . I feel . . ."

What? I wanted to shout. *What? What do you feel?*

"I feel like I've been waiting for you my entire life," Daniel said, then blushed furiously.

I stopped dancing. I couldn't move. I couldn't even breathe. Could he have said anything more perfect? All thoughts of Sage flew right out of my mind.

"Wow."

And then he smiled, solidifying my first heart attack, and pressed his lips to mine. It was the single most perfect kiss I had ever experienced. In that moment, I wasn't part of any squad or facing nationals the next day. I wasn't fighting with anybody. I wasn't uncertain about a thing. I didn't even care if he never called me his girlfriend. All that mattered in the world was Daniel. And he had already said it all.

• • •

I floated back to my room on a heart-shaped bubble. Daniel had wished me luck and hit me with another unbelievable kiss before we parted at the elevators. Bethany and Chuck had gone to check out the game room, having found that a great love of Ping-Pong was another thing they had in common. Everything was falling into place.

Of course, the second I opened the door to my room, the bubble burst. Waiting for me were Tara, Mindy, Whitney, Phoebe, Erin, Chandra and Jaimee, all of whom stopped talking when I walked into the room. The lights were dimmed and Tara was flitting about, lighting a bunch of stinky candles that had to be a fire hazard. What now? Were they going to sacrifice me to the cheerleading gods?

"Look who's here!" Tara exclaimed, placing her lighter wand on the windowsill.

"What's with the inferno?" I joked, hoping for levity.

"They're for luck," Chandra said with a small eye roll.

"Should have guessed." I dropped my purse and key card on the table by the door. I hovered there, arms crossed over my chest, and waited.

"Nice of you to grace us with your presence," Tara said, hands on her tiny hips.

"Tara, I thought we agreed not to be all sarcastic," Whitney said, pulling her legs up under her on the bed.

"You agreed?" I said, hot with humiliation. "So . . . what? You've all been talking about me all night?"

"It's not like that," Mindy said, standing.

"Okay, instead of sarcastic, I'll be blunt," Tara said, stepping toward me. Her Badtz Maru nightshirt had developed some kind of stain under one of the arms. "Are you trying to single-handedly take down this squad?"

All the air whooshed out of the room. "What?"

"First there's the hair. *Then* you're late to lunch . . ."

"That was just—"

"*Then* you stick around after practice not to work on your sorry-ass jumps, but to give the *Jersey* girls *tips*?" Tara ranted.

"Hey! They just asked me to—" I paused. "Wait a minute. How did you find out about that?"

"See? I *told* you guys she never would have admitted it to us. You were going to keep that little piece of subterfuge a secret, weren't you?" Tara demanded.

"Subterfuge, Tara? Really?" Whitney said.

Tara ignored her, keeping her eyes trained on me. "Too bad for you I overheard some of your big-haired, bad-ass Beavers gushing about how *fabulous* you are and what a tremendous *help* you were to them."

I'll admit it. I took a moment to feel good about that one. But only a moment.

"And now I hear you ditched dinner tonight to go out with Daniel Healy!" Tara finished, throwing her arms up and letting them slap down at her sides. "Interesting. My boyfriend is here as well, but somehow I managed to tear myself away from him for an hour and eat with the squad. What were you thinking?"

"Well, if you'd let me get a word in, maybe I'll tell you!" I shouted.

Everyone stared at me. All of them, even Mindy and Whitney, looked expectant. Like they were ready and willing for me to try to explain. How could no one understand this? How could no one see my take on things?

"You know what? Forget it," I said. "I don't have to explain myself to you guys."

"Uh . . . Annisa? I think maybe you should," Chandra said.

"I thought you were on my side," I replied.

"I am! About some things," Chandra replied. "But there *are* rules. You can't just do whatever you want. Especially not now."

"This is nationals," Erin said.

"If I hear one more person say that!" I said, my shoulder muscles coiling in frustration. "Like I don't *know* it's nationals."

"Well, you're kind of not acting like you know it," Jaimee said, with her apologetic face on. "If you don't mind me saying."

"Maybe I do mind," I said. "God! You guys are supposed to be my friends! We're not a cult! When I signed on to this squad, I really didn't think that my wardrobe, my mealtimes and my *hair* were going to be regulated."

I knew I was ranting. I did. But I was cornered and angry. I had never felt so abandoned and alone. Part of me wanted to back down. To just let things go back to the way they were. But this had all started when Tara decided unilaterally that I should dye my hair, and that was just wrong. The girl had to know she couldn't make me change who I was. She had to know she wasn't in charge of my life. A girl has to have *some* pride.

"You're on a team here, Gobooski. You're either with us or you're not," Tara said.

Some friends, I heard Gia say in my mind. Suddenly I felt like a moron for even standing here and taking this from them.

"Annisa, all the rules and the dressing alike and stuff is just for a few days," Mindy said. "Why are you acting like this?"

"Maybe because I thought I had friends and it turns out I don't," I replied. "I'm still an outsider to you guys. The non-blonde chick from Jersey. I heard what some of you were saying about my old squad. That's what you really think of me, isn't it?"

"What are you talking about?" Whitney asked.

"That I'm some loser brown-haired thug from a garbage dump," I replied.

"I apologized for what I said," Phoebe put in lamely.

"That doesn't change the fact that you said it," I replied. "Well, fine. Maybe I am. Maybe with the lateness and the ditching and everything, maybe I'm just being me."

Maybe I was. Maybe I wasn't. What did I want? Who did I want to be? Honestly, even I didn't know anymore, which was kind of freaking me out. Not that I would ever admit it.

"But you know what? Dyeing my hair blonde isn't going to change who I am," I continued. "You either want me the way I am or you don't. That's up to you guys to decide."

"You picked a really bad time to rebel, Annisa," Tara said.

"I'm not rebelling," I told her, staring her down. "In fact, for the first time since I've been here, I'm just being myself."

"This isn't you," Mindy said.

"Well, maybe you don't know me," I snapped, then instantly felt awful about it. Mindy looked away and I did too.

"Look, I think we should just all calm down and get a little sleep," Chandra suggested, sliding off the bed.

"You'll feel better in the morning, right, Annisa?" Jaimee said hopefully.

"It's almost curfew anyway," Erin said.

Curfew. Great. Another rule. I felt like all this stuff was just piling onto my shoulders, weighing me down.

I looked at all of them, at their disappointed and angry faces. The last thing I wanted to do was to crawl into bed with Mindy, who probably hated me now, and try to sleep in the same room with her and Tara and Phoebe. I didn't want to feel better in the morning. I wanted to feel better now.

I grabbed my key and whipped the door open.

"Annisa! If you walk out of here, you are in so much trouble!" Tara shouted.

I had no idea what to say in reply. I just knew I had to get away from them. I let the slamming door do the talking.

I could hear the laughter and music from all the way down the hall and I knew it was Becca and Gia throwing a little de-stress bash. If anyone knew how to have a good time, it was my old squad. I felt a smile spread across my face as I approached the door to Jordan's room. The Sand Dune Crabs could learn a few things from the Northwood Beavers. Like how to chill.

One rap on the door and the entire place went silent. I heard shushing and whispering and a few clinks as bottles were stashed under beds. How the heck did these people not get caught more often?

"What's the password?" Gia Kistrakis asked through the door.

The password? How had I forgotten about the password? "Uh . . . 'Kiss it'?"

The door flew open and cigarette smoke poured out. "That was the password, like, a year ago, Goober," Gia said, yanking me inside.

"You could have just checked the peephole," I said as I coughed up a lung.

"Annisa!" everyone cheered, raising soda cans and plastic cups.

I gave them a little wave and smiled. Donna Morales

reached under the bed and pulled out a large, half-full bottle of Southern Comfort and some smaller bottles of brown stuff I didn't recognize. Becca produced a bottle of vodka and some OJ from under the table. Somewhere in the vicinity was a liquor-store owner who had been taken in by Gia's seriously bad fake ID.

"You can never be too safe," Becca said, pushing herself up from the floor.

"Yeah, how do I know you haven't turned narc on us?" Gia asked. She took a long drag on her cigarette and blew smoke over my head.

"I haven't," I told her. Becca held a cup out to me and I lifted my hand. "No, thanks."

"She hasn't turned lush either," Becca joked, causing Gia to snicker.

"Are you sure you guys should be doing this?" I asked as I watched Christine Dent pour vodka into a cup of orange juice. "They have some serious rules and regulations at this thing."

"Still the goody-goody," Becca said, hooking her arm over my shoulder and turning me around. "Hey, Jordan! Your partner in innocence is here!"

A couple of girls catcalled me and I just rolled my eyes. I was used to being one of the few non-partiers in this particular crowd. In the past, Jordan, Maria and I had always stuck together at these types of soirees, just hunkering down with our sodas until it was over. Sure enough, Jordan and Maria were playing a game of Spit on the bed near the window with a couple of cans of Sprite nearby. Jordan lifted her chin at me, then went back to playing.

"Want a milk or something?" Gia teased, grabbing herself a cup.

"You need some new material," I teased back.

"You're lucky I have a buzz going or I might take offense to that," she told me.

I laughed and walked over to join Jordan and Maria. Their hands flew as they slapped cards down on the bedspread. Over the last couple of years we had all become serious Spit experts.

"Who's winning?" I asked, kneeling next to the bed.

"Isn't it obvious?" Jordan asked flatly.

I tried to read her face, but she wasn't looking at me. She was looking at the cards. It was clear Maria was kicking Jordan's butt. She had far fewer cards in front of her.

"Hey, could I talk to you for a second?" I asked Jordan.

"Kind of in the middle of something here . . . ," Jordan replied, slapping down card after card.

"Not anymore!" Maria shouted, throwing out her last card and putting her hands in the air. "I win."

"Ugh!" Jordan dropped what she was doing and flung herself back on the bed. "I've totally lost my Spit mojo."

"I'm gonna get another soda. You guys want?" Maria asked.

"I'm good," I replied.

"Nah," Jordan said, sitting up again and straightening the cards. "Wanna play?" she asked me.

"Actually, I kind of want to talk," I replied. I sat across from her cross-legged. "Is something wrong?"

"With me?" Jordan asked.

"Yeah. Well, no. I mean, *between* you and me," I said.

She was concentrating really hard on shuffling the cards. "You tell me."

"Jordan, come on," I said. "Something is clearly up. You haven't looked at me since I walked in here and then there was that face."

"What face?" she asked, her eyes flashing.

"That face at practice today," I said. "You looked at me like I was Clay Aiken or something." I expected her to laugh at the Clay reference, but she didn't. My heart plummeted. "Jordan?"

"All right, fine," she said finally, throwing her legs over the side of the bed. "It's just you've been acting so . . . superior."

I couldn't have been more stunned if she'd told me she *was* Clay Aiken. "What?"

"All you ever talk about is your squad and how great they are," she said with a shrug. "And then we're here and you're giving *us* tips? Like you're some kind of cheerleading goddess or something all of a sudden?"

"Jordan, please! You know I don't think I'm all that," I said. Tired and frustrated tears stung at my eyes. What was going on with everyone lately?

"You sure act like it," she said under her breath.

"What?"

"It's like you've been on this other squad for a few months and suddenly you're a whole different person," Jordan said.

That seemed to be the consensus today. My squad was mad because I refused to be just like them, and now Jordan was mad because she thought I was already *too* much like them.

162

I felt like my head was going to spin off like one of those propeller toys from trying to keep track of it all.

"Look, I only gave you guys tips because Becca asked me to," I said, trying to focus on the one argument I could definitely refute. "I would never have come over there if she hadn't asked me."

"She did?" Jordan asked, looking at me squarely for the first time.

"Yeah, I did," Becca said, stepping up to us. "Are you guys breaking up or something?" she asked, waving her cup around. "'Cause I always thought you made the cutest couple."

I shook my head at Becca's lame joke. "See? I was just doing what she asked me to do," I told Jordan.

"And everyone knows that no one turns me down," Becca said, taking a sip from her cup. "Well, if they're smart."

"Oh," Jordan said. "Sorry. I guess it was a misunderstanding."

"It's okay," I said, even though it kind of wasn't. How could she think I would be all high and mighty like that? Jordan knew me better than anyone.

"Hey, Gia! Turn that song up!" Becca called out. She danced away from us, joining the rest of the squad over by the window.

"So was that it?" I asked Jordan. "Was that all that was bothering you? 'Cause I was kind of getting a vibe even before then."

"Nope, no vibe!" Jordan said, brightening a bit.

"You're sure?"

"I'm just a little nervous about the competition, that's all," she told me. "If I'm vibe-y, that's all it is."

163

She was holding something back. I knew she was. They don't call us best friends for nothing.

"Well, I—"

Suddenly there was a very loud, very angry-sounding knock on the door. Gia slapped her hand down on the off button on her CD player and everyone else froze.

"Jordan? Gia? It's Coach Martinez. Open up!"

"Oh, crap!" Becca whispered.

Everyone started shoving cups and bottles back under the beds and into drawers. Maria threw the window open and fanned the drapes to try to clear the room of smoke. Coach knocked again. Everyone was wide-eyed. There was no way that anyone with a brain could miss what had been going on in here. The place was a mess and it reeked.

"We're so dead," Becca said. Her eyes fell on me. "Annisa, get out of here."

"Where do you want me to go?"

Christine opened a door that connected Jordan's room to the next one and waved me over. I looked at Jordan, who was pale as the sand outside.

"Go," she said, standing. "If we're going down, there's no reason to take you with us."

I had a sudden vision of Coach Holmes bursting into flame when the officials told her I was disqualified for smoking and drinking. The squad already hated me enough. As irritated as I was with them, I wasn't ready to throw all our hard work to the wolves.

"Good luck," I said. Then I slipped out of the room just as Coach Martinez started shouting at the others to open the door.

Christine and I and a bunch of the other girls from the Beavers closed the door behind us and snuck right over to the doorway that led to the hall. Christine opened it noiselessly and I peeked out. Becca had opened the door to their room and Coach looked like she was about to scream.

"One of the other squads complained about the noise coming from this room," Coach Martinez said to Becca. "Care to explain?"

"Was it the Black Bears?" Becca asked.

"Not that it matters, but yes," Coach said.

"Wow, they must have been dogs in another life," Gia said sarcastically. "They're two floors down from us. That's some serious hearing ability."

"Can it, Kistrakis," Coach Martinez said. "I think it's time we had a little talk."

Becca let her in and as soon as the door was closed, I waved at the others and slipped out into the hall. I raced to the stairwell and flung myself inside, petrified that I was about to hear Coach Martinez screech my name. Once I was safe and sound, however, I caught my breath and started down the stairs. I couldn't believe the Black Bears had reported the Beavers. But I guess Becca had given up the right to good sportsmanship when she'd tossed that girl in the pool. All was fair in love and cheerleading. I just hoped the Beavers didn't get in too much trouble.

I paused at my floor and opened the door, but a sizzle of trepidation shot through me. I really wasn't ready to go back to my room just yet, where everyone hated me. I glanced at my watch and sighed. It was past our curfew. I was already in trouble. Maybe I would go to Daniel's room and see if he was still up. I had been in such a good mood when I left him and I knew that hanging out with him would return me to cloud nine. Maybe if we hung out long enough, I could sneak back into the room after everyone was dead asleep.

I let the door close and headed downstairs.

Daniel and his roomies were, unfortunately, not in their room, so I headed for the lobby instead, thinking I might find them chilling down there. The place was still happening, but in a more hushed way than during the day. The guys weren't there, but I saw a few girls I recognized from lunch that day walking in through the front door with their parents. A bunch of cheerleaders in matching sweatshirts posed for a picture in front of the waterfall fountain across from the front desk. They threw their arms around each other and grinned. Somewhere nearby a team was chanting and laughing. Just listening to all the cheer made my heart hurt.

Feeling heavy and low, I dropped into one of the vacant chairs and slumped. This was not how this competition was supposed to go. I should have been hanging out with my squad, having a good time, bonding and laughing and chanting and being silly. Instead I was all alone in the lobby, being pathetic.

I heard a familiar voice and looked up to find Steven shaking hands with an older, athletic-looking couple. He pocketed his tape recorder and made a note on a notepad as the pair walked away. Someone was working late.

"Hey! Steven!" I called out, desperate for a little company.

His face lit up when he saw me. It made me feel a little better. I hadn't been getting that reaction a whole lot today.

"Annisa! What's going on?" he asked, crossing the room. "Where is everybody?"

"In bed. We have a curfew, remember?"

"So . . . what are you doing here?" he asked.

"Being bad to the bone," I joked lamely. "Who were those people?"

"I was just interviewing a couple of the judges," Steven told me, sitting down on the coffee table across from me. He placed his vinyl backpack next to him. "I wanted to get an idea of how this whole competition thing works."

"And? What do you think?" I asked.

"I think you guys are in for it," Steven said incredulously. "These people do not mess around. They score on the difficulty, the precision, the enthusiasm, the *music*. Did you know they score on the music?"

"Yeah. Most squads get theirs professionally mixed," I said. "Luckily for our budget, Coach's boyfriend is a DJ."

"Sweet," Steven said. "I'll have to put that in the article. Maybe I can profile him." He whipped out his notepad and jotted a few things down.

"Well, I guess I'll leave you and your notepad alone," I said, hoisting myself up.

"No, wait," Steven said. He flipped the pad closed and put it down. "Hey. Is something wrong? You look a little, I don't know, not happy."

"Crack investigative journalism," I joked, falling back into the chair.

"What's up?" he asked, clearly concerned.

"Off the record?" I asked.

"Do you even have to ask anymore?" he asked me, lifting his hands, palm up.

I stared him down. "Yuh-huh I have to ask. Skirt? Over head? On front page?"

"Okay, off the record," he said finally.

"Well, let's just say I am not having fun here," I said.

"How is that possible?" Steven asked. "You're here with the squad. Your *old* friends are here. I saw Bethany this afternoon. It's like a playground for Annisa."

I scoffed. "I wish."

Steven watched me steadily as if he were waiting for me to say something else. Finally the intensity of the stare started to freak me out and I became very intent on flicking my key card back and forth on the back of my hand.

"Want to go for a walk on the beach?" Steven asked. "Fresh air could help."

I practically jumped out of my chair. "Let's go."

We walked out the back door of the hotel. The pool glowed with the help of underwater lights and the waterfall sounded a lot louder when there weren't dozens of gabbing girls around. As we approached the beach, we saw a couple walking along the water's edge, hand in hand, and we both automatically turned in the other direction. I slipped my sandals off and let my bare feet sink into the cool sand.

"So, what's going on? Off the record," Steven added quickly.

"Well, let's see . . . . My new squad wants to give me a dye job and throw in a personality removal for free," I said, swinging my sandals as I walked. "Meanwhile, my best friend from home thinks I've already had one. A personality removal, not a dye job."

"Harsh," Steven said.

"I just feel like I'm under the microscope all the time," I told him. "If I say one thing wrong, everyone jumps all over me."

"That's not a good feeling," Steven said. He pulled his bag around his side and started rummaging through it.

"You're not taking out your tape recorder, are you?" I asked.

"Please! Me? Record a woman in pain?" He pulled out a bag of peanut M&M's and handed them to me. "*This* is what you need."

I grinned. "You sure you don't want them?"

"They're all yours," he said, smiling.

Never one to turn down chocolate in a time of crisis—or any other time, actually—I tore into the bag and popped a couple of M&M's into my mouth. Ah. The world looked so much brighter with a mouthful of chocolaty peanut goodness.

"Better?" he asked.

I nodded. I couldn't speak without showering him with peanut bits.

"Good, 'cause I have some advice," he said. "Do you want my advice?"

"Sure," I managed to say.

"It sounds to me like you're caught between two worlds— your old one and your new one. And you want to be in both places. You can't decide where you belong. Am I right?" he asked.

I thought it over. "I guess . . ."

"Well, when it comes down to it, you don't really have much choice," he said, pausing in the soft sand. "You live in

Florida now. This is your world," he said, spreading his arms.

I looked around at the beach and the reeds and the sparkling hotel just beyond. It didn't *feel* like my world. It felt more like a dream. Something temporary.

"Maybe you just haven't accepted that yet," Steven said. "Maybe you have to come to terms with the fact that it's time to leave your old life behind. You can't move back, you know. Only forward."

I looked at him, my brow creasing in thought. He had a point. Unfortunately most of the people I was supposed to be moving forward with currently hated my guts. "What are you, a teen shrink?" I asked.

"No, but both my parents are," he said with a grin. "Shrinks, not teens."

"That explains it," I said, popping another M&M.

"Well, once you accept the fact that Sand Dune is your home, I think you'll have no problem figuring out who you're going to be there," he said, taking a step closer to me. "For the record, whoever you've been since you got here, I really like her."

"Thanks," I said, swallowing. "That's really nice of y—"

I never got to finish my sentence because, I swear on my life, Steven Schwinn leaned forward and planted a big old wet one right on my lips. And I mean *big* and *wet*.

What was he *doing?* That was my first reaction. My second reaction was a series of flashing images through my mind. Steven waiting for me outside the locker room, asking my dad all kinds of personal questions about me. And what had he done with the answers he'd gotten? He'd used them.

He had Beatles music on the bus. He had M&M's in his bag at the ready. And hadn't he been wearing a whole lot of red ever since I told him it was my favorite color?

I yanked my face away from him and stumbled backward, wiping the back of my hand across my mouth. Steven looked startled. I searched for something to say. At that exact moment, I heard a few male voices up the beach near the path that led back to the hotel. I looked up, my heart pounding, to see Bobby Goow, Christopher Healy, Carlos Verde and, yes, Daniel Healy, all clambering onto the beach. Well, the first three were clambering and laughing and shoving each other around. Daniel was just standing there, staring at me like he had just lost his best friend.

In a rush of realization, I knew he had seen me. He had seen me getting a saliva bath from Steven Schwinn. Oh . . . my . . . God!

"Daniel!"

He turned around and bolted as if the sound of his name was actually a gunshot. I dropped the M&M's and took off after him, but I had a lot of beach to cover and it was slow going. By the time I reached the pathway, Daniel had already rounded the pool and was heading into the hotel.

"Annisa!" Steven called after me. "Where are you going?"

I ignored him. Steven I could deal with later. Right now I was not going to lose Daniel.

I sprinted around the pool, my bare feet slapping against the concrete. "Daniel!" I shouted.

He slowed down as he reached the back door and I finally caught up with him. He whipped around so quickly, I almost lost my balance. I stopped and held my hand over my heart, totally out of breath. Between the sprint and the desperation I was going to be needing a defibrillator any second.

"I knew it!" he said loudly. "I knew there was something going on between you two!"

"What?" I gasped.

"You and Steven Schwinn!" Daniel said through his teeth. I had never seen him so emotional before. Not even when he had caught Sage cheating on him with Gabe and he had shoved my brother into a garbage bag full of beer cans. "I can't believe I drove all the way down here for someone who's cheating on me! First Sage and now you!"

I don't know if it was shock at the level of his anger, or disgust over being compared to Sage, but I could not find my tongue. It was nowhere in my mouth. It had entirely left my body.

"I'm such an idiot!" Daniel said, pushing his hand into his hair.

"I . . . I wasn't cheating on you," I said finally. But between the breathlessness and the confusion, it didn't sound that convincing. Even to me.

"Are you kidding me?" Daniel said, throwing his arm out toward the beach. "I just saw you! I saw you with my own eyes! He had his tongue halfway down your throat!"

I shuddered at the memory and Daniel took the opportunity to turn on his heel and storm into the lobby. Suddenly I felt my face heat up with irritation. Yet another person refused to see my side of things. What was with everybody? I yanked the door open and followed him.

"Hey! Aren't you even going to give me a chance to explain?" I shouted at his back.

He tipped his head back, then turned around. "Explain what?"

"What just happened!" I said. "All we did was go for a walk on the beach. It's not like I *expected* him to kiss me!"

He scoffed. "A walk on the beach in the dark. What else was going to happen, Annisa?"

I narrowed my eyes at his condescension. "You were out there with Bobby and Carlos and your brother! Planning on kissing any of them?"

He took a deep breath. "Great. You cheated on me and now you're making jokes?"

I couldn't take it anymore. He kept throwing the word *cheat* at me when *he* was the one talking to Sage in the hallway and letting her touch his hair and maybe calling her and then lying about it. Where did he get off calling me a cheat?

"Forget it," he said, turning and striding into the lobby.

"Fine! Believe what you want to believe!" I shouted after him, stopping at the edge of the shining lobby floor. "But you can't cheat on someone you're not technically going out with!"

The few people left in the lobby all turned to gape at me. A couple of girls sipping coffees at a table shot me a look like I was completely pathetic. Daniel stopped for a split second. I stared at his back, willing him to turn around. Hoping there was some way for us to erase everything and go back to that last good-night kiss we had shared a little over an hour ago. It was almost impossible to believe that earlier tonight I had been floating—that earlier tonight everything had been perfect.

Daniel did turn around, but all he did was shoot me a look that was full of hurt and betrayal. Then he kept walking and never turned back again.

"Stop, stop, stop!" Coach Holmes shouted, waving her hands at us.

Everyone groaned and paused mid–dance move as she killed the music. I stood off to the side, conspicuous. I knew I had screwed up the sequence. I had skipped about five moves and gone right into the domino jumps. The fact that the rest of the team was crouched on the floor while I was three feet above it kind of tipped me off.

Get your head in the game, Annisa, I told myself. Of course, considering I had barely slept and I was still really upset over a number of cataclysmic events, the game was not a place my head was willing to be. A pillow was what it really needed.

"Annisa, what is going on with you this morning?" Coach asked.

Over on the other side of the room, the Black Bears stopped practicing long enough to point and snicker. Loved those girls. Really. *Loved* them.

"Sorry, Coach," I said, looking at the floor. I could feel at least a dozen angry glares boring into the back of my neck.

"She was probably too busy staying up all night giving pointers to all the other squads," Sage muttered under her breath, causing Lindsey to snort a laugh.

I could have pulled her hair. Really. She was that irritating.

"Sorry doesn't cut it today," Coach said, standing in front of me with her arms crossed over her chest. "We have prelims in an hour. You need to step it up. Now."

"Got it," I said.

She eyed me curiously, then lowered her voice. "Everything okay with you, Gobrowski? Did you sleep all right?"

Wow. I must have even *looked* exhausted.

"Not really," I admitted.

Coach placed her hand on my back and rubbed it around in a comforting way. "I know these things can be nerve-racking. Why don't you go get yourself some juice or coffee and try to perk up? We need you at full energy for this thing."

"Okay, Coach," I said, mustering a smile. "Thanks."

"Anytime."

At least *she* didn't hate me.

"All right, everyone, that's enough for now," Coach Holmes called out. "Let's all take a break. We'll meet back here at 11:45 for stretching and the power circle."

A few of my teammates clapped and cheered, but most of them just grabbed their stuff and hustled out of the room. I wasn't surprised that no one stuck around to give me a pep talk. Barely anyone had spoken to me at breakfast either. Apparently they were all really annoyed when they heard about me helping the Beavers. I was a leper all over again.

I hoisted my bag onto my shoulder and was about to head for the café when Tara stepped in front of me. She did not look like she was in a pep-talky kind of mood either. Fantastic.

"We need to talk," she said.

Talking was basically the last thing I wanted to do, but I knew I couldn't avoid her forever. I decided to stand my ground. Maybe Tara would have something constructive to say.

"Okay," I replied, lifting my chin.

"I don't know why Coach is going easy on you, but as far as I'm concerned, your performance is your own fault," she said, her eyes sharp.

Or maybe not.

"I really don't need this right now," I said, starting past her.

"You're the one who missed curfew," Tara said, calling after me. "If we go down today, it's on you."

"Fine!" I said, lifting my arm with my back to her.

Nice captain. I was starting to think she had been voted into the position only because everyone was afraid of her. Clearly she knew nothing about rallying the troops or having compassion. She knew even less about taking responsibility. All she had ever done since I arrived in Sand Dune was pin stuff on me. My eyes filled with tears of exhaustion and frustration.

As I walked out of the ballroom, I glanced at the Beavers, who were going over their final pyramid. Jordan was at the top of the structure, arms in a perfect high V, smile wide, staring straight ahead. They all looked happy and energetic and raring to go. Surprising, considering their night of debauchery. But at least they were still here. At least Coach Martinez hadn't decided to punish them by sending them home.

And at least they appeared to be having fun. That was a lot more than I could say for my squad.

. . .

Backstage before the semifinal performances was a dizzying flurry of activity. Some squads went over their routines, doing the moves small and tight, counting out their eight-counts under their breath. Other squads sat in clumps, holding hands, saying prayers. Still others ran around making last-minute adjustments on their hair and uniforms.

Autumn, Chandra and I sat on a bench near the wall while the rest of our squad stood in front of us, mingling, trying to talk about anything but what we were about to do. We had drawn a late number, so there were ten squads up before us. It was a good idea to try to get our minds off things in the meantime. Autumn and Chandra were two of the very few squad members who hadn't frozen me out and I was happy that I still had someone to talk to.

Surprisingly, Mindy was still talking to me, but only when necessary. She was the only person whose actions I truly understood. I still couldn't believe I had snapped at her the way I had. Sooner or later I was going to have to apologize. I just hadn't had a chance to get her alone yet. That was the problem with being on a squad of sixteen.

"How much longer do you think it'll be?" I asked.

Autumn looked at the clock on the opposite wall. "At least another half hour."

"I have to pee!" some girl squealed to her friend, rushing by us.

"You can't pee now! We're up next!" the friend shouted.

"If I don't pee now, I'm gonna pee on your head!" the first girl shouted back.

Chandra and I looked at each other and cracked up laugh-

ing. Autumn squirmed. "Oh, Goddess. Now I have to pee."
She jumped up and ran for the bathroom.

"Wow. I never thought I would be this intimately aware
of my friends' bodily functions," I joked, taking a slug of
water.

"We all get our period at the same time too, you know,"
Chandra replied, her heels bouncing up and down under her
chair. "Have you noticed?"

"Um, no," I said. "But now I'm sure I will."

"Up next, the Marshall High School Cowgirls!" the back-
stage coordinator shouted, temporarily silencing the room.
Talk about power. "On deck, the Northwood High School
Beavers!"

My heart skipped a nervous beat and I saw the Beavers
all exchange excited glances.

"I'll be back," I told Chandra.

"Going to give your little friends some last-minute
advice?" Sage called after me. A few of my squad mates
snickered. My shoulder muscles coiled, but I managed to
ignore them.

The Beavers were making their way toward the wings and
I joined them. Jordan grinned when she found me by her
side. She was clutching her lucky Derek Jeter pen in both
hands. Jordan was a huge Jeter fan and a couple of summers
ago she had basically accosted him outside Yankee Stadium
and gotten him to sign a baseball for her. This was the pen
he had used. It had brought us both luck ever since.

"Is this actually happening?" Jordan asked.

"Yep. But don't worry. You guys look great," I said.

"Yeah. We clean up good," Gia said.

And they did. Their competition uniforms were a deep red with white and gold stripes crisscrossing the top and the word BEAVERS spelled across the chest. The skirts were super straight with matching stripes running down the side. They all had their hair pulled back in perfect French braids. There wasn't an ounce of gold jewelry or glittered nail polish in sight. I had never seen my old squad looking so crisp and - clean-cut.

"Can you believe how many people are out there?" Jordan asked. "What is this, the World Series?"

"May as well be," I said.

"Great. I'm not nervous enough," Jordan said with a smile.

"You're gonna do awesome," I told her. "Just get out there and kick a little ass."

The crowd went nuts for the Marshall High team and a guy with a headset stuck his face around the red curtain. "All right, Beavers. You're up in thirty seconds."

"Omigod," Jordan said. She looked like she was about to throw up.

"Uh . . . better let me take that," I said, going for the pen. I had to pry it out of her cold-as-ice hands.

"Right," she said with a laugh. "Can't cheer with that."

"I'll take good care of it," I said.

"I know. Thanks, Annisa," she replied. She grabbed me up in a quick, tight hug and I almost burst into tears. "I'm glad you're here," she said.

"Me too," I replied. "Break a leg!"

"All right, Beavers! Huddle up!" Becca shouted as the Marshall team bounded by us from the stage.

All the girls in red formed a tight klatch and I stepped

back, feeling hollow inside. I wasn't a Beaver anymore. They were going out there without me. It felt like I was moving away all over again.

"And now, from the state of New Jersey, the Northwood High School Beavers!" the announcer called out.

Jordan and the others raced out onto the mat, throwing their arms in the air and cheering their hearts out. It was so exciting, just to see them out there. I grinned through my jealousy and stepped as close to the stage as Mr. Headset would allow. This was one performance I was not going to miss.

• • •

The Beavers opened a can of whoop-ass out on that mat. They were awesome. Not one screwup as far as I could see, and even Gia's faces were flawless. If the Beavers didn't make the top ten, I was going to be shocked.

Wow. There was one sentence I never thought I'd say. They had really come a long way.

Minutes after the Beavers raced off the mats, I bounded out from behind the curtains with my new squad. As miffed as I had felt all morning, there was no denying the excitement coursing through my veins at that moment. This was nationals. The crowd was intense. My whole squad had so much energy, we were like a kindergarten class on cupcake day. I took my place in the opening formation and told myself to forget about the last twenty-four hours. To pretend this was just last week's game when I was so excited about cheerleading and I loved my squad and I couldn't wait to get here.

I looked up at the crowd. My parents had told me they were going to try to sit on the left side near the top, but I couldn't find them. I did, however, see Daniel sitting there with his brother and the other guys, wearing WHADDUP SAND

181

DUNE? T-shirts. My heart gave a lurch. He was still here. He hadn't fled for home. That had to be a good sign, right?

Now my mind was off in Daniel La-La Land, so when the music started up, it took me by surprise. Not enough to throw me off, though. I flung myself into the routine like I never had before. This was the biggest competition of our lives. As they say, it was time to bring it.

As I popped up into my first toss, I heard the crowd gasp and then cheer. I kept my eyes on the judges as I came down and did my first jump. I swear they exchanged impressed glances. The smile that was already glued to my face widened as we launched into our first major dance sequence. The audience was loving the music, dancing in their seats and clapping along. Then it was time for the cheer portion. I popped up into the air in Autumn and Chandra's palms. The crowd looked even bigger from up there.

"All you fans, yell 'Go!'"

"Go!"

I thrust my sign to the sky and I swear the shouting almost knocked me over.

"All you fans, yell 'Crabs!'"

"Crabs!"

Oh yeah, they liked us. They really liked us.

By the time the routine was done, I was out of breath, but confident. I hadn't messed up once. Not a single time. There was absolutely nothing Tara Timothy could say to me.

Everyone hugged and cheered and laughed as we raced backstage. Whitney grabbed me in her ridiculously toned arms and spun me around. Coach Holmes jogged over, beaming.

"That was incredible, girls! You're a lock!"

We all cheered and squealed, and then I heard it. Sage's voice. She was jumping up and down, talking to Maureen.

"He's here! I knew it! I knew he'd come!" she said giddily.

My heart turned to stone. She had seen Daniel in the crowd too. I *knew* it. I *knew* she wanted him back.

"Um . . . Annisa?" Mindy said, undoubtedly noticing the complete transformation in my face.

I barely heard her. My sights were set on Sage like a bitch-seeking missile system. I slipped by the other girls and tapped her on the shoulder. Sage turned around and the expression of elation slid right off.

"Just so you know, he's here to see me, not you," I said. "He came to take me out to dinner last night, so maybe you should just wake up and smell the reality already."

"Ooooh." That was my teammates. Yeah, that's right. Don't mess with Annisa Gobrowski.

Sage just looked confused. Probably not used to me standing up for myself without getting all tongue-tied and hyper. I was as cold as granite.

It was really pretty cool, if I do say so myself.

"What are you—"

"Excuse me?" Coach Holmes interrupted, stepping up in front of me. "*That's* why you missed dinner last night? I was told you were throwing up from nerves."

My foot dove directly into my mouth. Tara Timothy hung her head. Whitney covered her eyes with her hand. That big old vein in Coach's forehead was visibly throbbing.

Order me up a wreath of roses. I was dead.

Okay, saying that I had skipped dinner for Daniel in front of the entire squad might not have been the best idea, but I'd assumed they already knew. Can you blame me? Phoebe and Mindy were so mad at me when I bailed with Bethany and Daniel, I figured they must have told the rest of the squad. Tara, Jaimee, Chandra and Erin sure seemed to know last night. That was almost half of them right there!

But I guess I should have known they wouldn't tell Coach. No matter what the situation, there was still some solidarity among teammates when it came to dealing with adults. Duh.

"Gobrowski, we need to talk," Coach Holmes said.

"Coach, come on. It's really not that big of a deal, is it?" Chandra asked, coming to my defense. I found myself stepping closer to her side. "I mean, it was only one meal. And the food kind of sucked anyway."

"I second that," Whitney said, making a grossed-out face.

"That's really not the point, Albohm," Coach said.

"She's right," Erin piped in. "Annisa disrespected all of us by skipping out on a meal for a guy."

"Exactly," Jaimee said.

"Well, what's one meal in the face of true love?" Autumn

countered. "It must have been so romantic, him coming down here to sweep you away."

If only it had *ended* so romantically.

"Well, that's true too," Jaimee said, looking pained. "It was only one dinner . . ."

"Jaimee, are you even capable of making up your mind?" Erin snapped.

"Hey!" Jaimee said. "I'm just being diplomatical."

"You mean diplomatic," Felice put in.

"I hate how you're always correcting me," Jaimee said, whirling on Felice. "Just 'cause you got into Penn State early decision—"

"U Penn!" Felice replied. "It's an Ivy League, okay? Penn State is a hole in the ground."

"As a Penn State alumnus, I'd just like to say—watch it," Coach Holmes told her.

Felice turned ten shades of purple. "Sorry, Coach."

"Well, whatever, maybe I get words mixed up sometimes, but that's no reason to make me feel stupid!" Jaimee said. "You know I got a perfect score on my math PSAT? What did you get?"

Felice's jaw dropped. "I . . . Really?"

"We're getting away from the point here," Erin said. "And the point is—"

"That Annisa's our teammate and we should let *her* explain," Chandra said.

"She already tried that last night," Erin countered. "And can I just say that I don't think the Daniel thing is *half* as bad as her giving up tips to the enemy."

"You go, girl!" Sage said as the rest of the team grumbled their agreement.

186

"What?" Coach Holmes blurted.

"They're not the enemy!" I cried. "And I was just—"

"Being more loyal to them than you are to us," Erin interrupted.

My face burned as the entire team started talking over one another.

"I think that we should all—"

"No one cares what you think—"

"Everyone just breathe. Serenity, people! Serenity—"

"Oh, stuff the serenity, Autumn."

Suddenly there was a loud, sharp whistle and my heart leapt in surprise. Everyone turned to look at Tara, who was standing next to Whitney, she of the perfect two-fingered whistle.

"Enough!" Tara shouted. "I am still the captain of this squad and I want everyone to shut up and calm down. You're making a scene."

I glanced over my shoulder and sure enough, a bunch of the other squads were all huddled up, watching us.

"Any second now they're going to call us out there to announce the finalists, and you will all be smiling and happy or I swear to God I will personally find a way to make each and every one of you regret it, got me?" she said through her teeth.

No one said a word. In my mind's eye I saw Tara flipping through FBI files on the squad members, wickedly discerning the specific methods for torturing each of her teammates.

"Everyone listen up!" the backstage manager shouted. He was already going hoarse from the effort of screaming over hundreds of cheerleaders. "I want the squads to line up in the following order for your entrance. First, right here by the curtains, the Marshall High Cowgirls . . . second, the Northwood High Beavers . . . third, the Sand Dune High Fighting Crabs . . ."

Even with all the insanity, my skin sizzled with anticipation. We were about to find out if we had made the top ten. Of course, win or lose, it seemed like nothing was ever going to be the same again. It kind of put a damper on things, to say the least.

"Let's go," Tara said.

"I'll deal with you later," Coach Holmes told me.

I turned and trudged into line. Autumn slipped her slim arm over my shoulders. "Finding serenity is important," she said morosely.

"I know," I told her, patting her on the back. "I know."

• • •

Gathered on the stage, I knelt in a line with seven other girls, while eight more stood behind us. Everyone was clutching hands, so we all did too, even though most of us probably didn't feel like it after that argument. Keeping the grin on my face was hard work. Between the nervousness over whether we made it and the palpable tension on the squad, smiling was the last thing on my mind. It made my cheek muscles hurt and turned the insides of my lips dry.

Gracie Beck, the former gymnast turned competition announcer, took the stage in her perfect blue suit and heels. Her formerly tiny body had filled out considerably since her Olympic days and her red hair was styled into a short, chic bob. I wondered what she would have said if her eight-member gold medal team had told her to dye that gorgeous hair to match theirs. She probably would have told them what they could do with their balance beams.

"First of all, I'd like to thank everyone here for an amazing competition, one of the best we've ever had," Gracie said into the microphone, clutching a large light blue index card. The announcement was met with insane applause.

"Of course, only ten squads can make it through to the finals and I know that if I put it off any longer, you might rebel on me." (Polite, nervous laughter.) "So without further ado, our first squad is . . ."

Chandra's grip on my fingers tightened.

"Well, this is no surprise. Last year's champions, the Mecatur High School Black Bears from Louisiana!"

On the opposite side of the stage, the Black Bears flipped out. Like to the point where it was scary. I thought one of them was going to pull something, she was jumping up and down so hard. I scanned the crowd again to keep from staring the Black Bears down and finally found my parents. My mom waved and my dad snapped a picture. Gabe was kicked back in his seat, buffing his fingernails. Yes, that was my brother.

Daniel was only a few rows ahead of them. I couldn't tell whether he was looking at me or Sage. Either way, he didn't look all that happy to be there.

"Congratulations, girls. Our next finalist squad is the Holy Cross High School Angels of California!"

Another squad in white, gold and black went nuts. My heart slammed around in my rib cage. Only eight squads left.

"If they made it, we definitely made it," Phoebe said behind me. "Did you see their stunts?"

"Pitiful," Whitney agreed.

"Bad luck!" Tara admonished them.

"Omigod, get over it," Whitney told her. "I can smell your feet from here."

I tried not to laugh. Two more teams were announced. Two more squads went ballistic. My palms were sweating so much that it was impossible to tell where my perspiration ended and Chandra's and Autumn's began.

"Number five," Gracie announced. "A brand-new entry at nationals this year, from right here in the great state of Florida, the Sand Dune High School Fighting Crabs!"

Before I knew it, I was on my feet. Everyone was hugging and bouncing and screaming. For that split second of psychotic happiness, everything was forgotten. I hugged everyone in sight. I think I even hugged Sage.

Once we calmed down and got back to our places, my heart felt a hundred times lighter than it had just moments ago. We were through to the finals. It was such a load off. Of course, I still had a lecture coming at me. And a squad full of people who hated me. And Daniel and Sage. And Jordan . . . and . . . *Jordan.*

I glanced left at the Beavers squad, all of whom had gone green from the effort of keeping up the smiles. Gracie Beck had called at least eight squads by now, and the Beavers weren't one of them.

Come on, I thought, mentally willing Gracie to read their name. *Come on! They were incredible! They* have *to make finals!*

"Our ninth squad is . . . the Southeast High School Lions of Tennessee!"

I applauded as the Tennessee squad freaked out. I hadn't really talked to any of them, but they were always polite when we were practicing, unlike another squad we shared a ballroom with.

"And last, but certainly not least . . . ," Gracie said.

The Northwood High School Beavers . . . the Northwood High School Beavers . . . the—

"Another new entry this year, the Northwood High School Beavers of New Jersey!" Gracie read.

"Oh my God!" I shouted.

Jordan and the others went super hyper crazy and I jumped to my feet and ran over to hug my best friend. They were in! I couldn't believe that both my squads were in the finals!

"Congratulations!" I shouted to the Beavers.

"You too!" Jordan shouted back.

Suddenly the stage was awash with color as squads intermingled, patting each other on the back or commiserating over being cut. The crowd started to thin out as parents found their kids and boyfriends hugged girlfriends. I had planned to meet my parents later, so I knew they weren't fighting their way toward the mat. I searched for Daniel in the crowd, but didn't see him. Meanwhile, people I had never met from squads I didn't know were congratulating me and wishing me luck. It was so nuts that for a second I forgot that I was in deep trouble.

But only for a second.

"I think your squad is waiting for you," Jordan said in my ear as we made our way backstage.

Sure enough, the whole team, along with Coach Holmes, was standing near the wall, talking in low tones.

"I'll catch you later," I said to Jordan.

As I made my way over to the squad, I saw Steven snapping pictures of them. Steven. I had almost forgotten about his role in the current mess. He lowered the camera and eyed me meaningfully. Like he wanted to talk.

Then Daniel and his friends stepped into the backstage area from a side door. Carlos ran right over to Erin and gave her a huge kiss. Bobby Goow enveloped Tara in his beefy arms. But Daniel . . . Daniel just stood there and eyed me meaningfully. Like he wanted to talk too.

I was totally trapped. Maybe I could just have them duel over me. I pictured Daniel and Steven in tights and capes, parrying back and forth with swords, swinging from the rafters in my name. Of course, at the moment it was possible that only one of them was in a fight-for-Annisa place. The wrong one.

"Come on, Gobrowski," Coach Holmes said, breaking away from the crowd. "Let's find someplace quiet."

Well, there was a way out. What was that saying? From the frying pan into the fire? Still, I had never been so happy to be in trouble in my life. Getting a smackdown from Coach Holmes was going to be a lot easier than sorting stuff out with Daniel and Steven.

I glanced over my shoulder as Coach led me to a back hallway. And wouldn't you know it? Daniel was now talking with none other than Sage Barnard. I felt my blood boil. That girl *really* did not know when to quit. It was all I could do to keep from turning around, marching back there and hitting her with an atomic wedgie.

Actually, just the mental image was rather satisfying.

"Gobrowski, I . . . are you smiling?" Coach asked, appalled.

"Sorry, Coach," I said.

She crossed her arms over her chest and shook her head. "I swear, I'm beginning to think I don't even know who you are," she said. "Skipping out on a team meal at nationals? Lying to your teammates? When you first joined this squad, I thought you were the most dedicated cheerleader I had ever seen."

Really? I thought.

"You worked your butt off to catch up with the others. You dealt with all their crap. But now? Honestly? If we weren't in the middle of an important competition, I'd have half a mind to bench you," she said. "This is not Annisa Gobrowski behavior."

I swallowed hard and looked at my sneakers. When it came to being brought back to earth, there was nothing like a person you really admired telling you how much you had disappointed them. She was right, of course. This *wasn't* Annisa Gobrowski behavior. But I knew that already. Unfortunately, I was having a hard time figuring out *who* I was and *what* I wanted to do. I wanted to be a good teammate, but my current teammates weren't making it easy for me. I wanted to be a good friend, but it seemed next to impossible to be a good friend to everyone without offending somebody. And how was I supposed to be me when everything I wanted to do seemed to annoy at least some of the people I cared about?

I just wanted someone to tell me what to do. Tell me what was right and what was wrong. If I kept trying to figure it out myself, I was definitely going to rupture something.

"Did you see how everyone was fighting before?" Coach said to me. "This is a really bad time for this team to unravel. Now, you brought them together once before, Annisa. I'm counting on you to be part of the solution again, not part of the problem."

My feet felt wet in my sneakers. I shivered and became acutely aware of all my exposed skin, to the point where I had to hug myself to keep from shaking. "Yes, Coach."

"And whatever this crap is about giving tips to other teams, that ends now," Coach added. "I'm all for being a good sport, but this *is* a competition. Your loyalty should be to one squad and one squad only, are we clear?"

"Yes, Coach."

"Good, because if you step so much as a toe out of line again on this trip, I'll have no problem replacing you when we get back to Sand Dune," she said.

Wow. Don't pull any punches. "Yes, Coach," I said.

"Okay then. We understand each other. Now, everyone is meeting up with their families for lunch today, but I *will* see you at dinner."

With that, she walked off, leaving me alone in the hallway. Suddenly feeling exhausted, I leaned back against the wall and took a deep breath. This competition was definitely not turning out like I had imagined. I had pictured excitement, laughter, tons of happy, smiling pictures with my friends.

Instead, I was more miserable than I had ever been in my entire life.

By the time I changed my clothes and got back downstairs to meet my family for lunch, the sky had turned gray and it looked like rain. A stiff wind had kicked up and all the squads that had packed for Southern Florida temps were emptying the gift shop of its sweatshirts. It definitely felt more like New Jersey than Florida. I actually found it sort of comforting.

Already there was a huge banner strung across the front of the lobby that read "Congratulations, Finalists!" Underneath, all the top-ten teams were listed in our school colors. These cheerleading organizations were definitely on top of things.

"You look . . . cozy," my mother said to me as I trudged over to her. Gabe and my father were chatting with some guy at the front desk.

I was wearing my favorite baggy jeans and an old, tattered Rutgers University sweatshirt. My hair was pulled back under a bandana. All makeup and hairspray had been removed. The standard uniform of the depressed. The only traces of my Florida wardrobe were my comfy red flip-flops and the blue toenails Mindy and I had painted last week for extra school spirit.

"A girl can only coif so much," I told her.

"I hear that," she said, slipping her arm over my shoulders. "Is everything all right with you? You looked a little strained out there on the floor today."

Whoa. Everything welled up inside of me so fast, I thought I was going to gush from every pore. What was it about Mom's voice that made me ache to spill my guts?

But I couldn't. I already felt like I had been through an emotional wringer over the past couple of days. All I wanted was to have a nice, laid-back lunch with my family. So I put on a happy face.

"Just a little worn-out from all the rah-rah craziness," I said with a shrug. "All I need is a big burger and some fries and I'll be back to my old self again."

"I think we can accommodate that request," my father said, joining us. "We got a list of restaurants from the front desk and one of them claims to have the best burgers in the state. Shall we try them out?"

"As long as I can get some grilled chicken there," Gabe said. "I'm watching my carbs."

"The pizza prince of the tristate area is watching his carbs?" I asked.

That's not a made-up title. The manager of the Domino's in my old hometown threw Gabe a party when he ordered his three hundredth pie. They gave him a crown and everything. As far as I know, his picture is still hanging on the wall.

"Ugh! I haven't had a pizza in weeks," Gabe said, pulling a face. He turned to a mirror near the front desk, touched his fingertip to his tongue, and used it to smooth his eyebrow.

I looked at my parents, feeling a little skeeved. "Have you guys taken him for an MRI yet?"

"Believe me, I'm thinking about it," my father said, eyeing my brother like he was a Martian.

Across the lobby I saw Whitney and Sage with their parents, chatting with Mindy and her dad. Erin and Carlos joined a woman who was either Erin's older sister or her very in-shape and moisturized mom. Phoebe stepped out of the elevator and paused when she saw us.

"Phoebe! Hi! How's it going?" my brother asked with a huge smile.

He was definitely using some kind of whitener. Can you say blinding?

"Hi, Gabe!" Phoebe said with a little smile. "Mr. and Mrs. Gobrowski."

"Nice to see you again, Phoebe," my mother said. "We were just going out for burgers. Would you like to come?"

"Uh . . . thanks," Phoebe said, twisting the hem of her sweatshirt in her hands. She had yet to even look at me. "But I have . . . other plans."

"Of course," my dad said. "Good to . . . ."

But the rest of the sentence was lost on Phoebe, who had hurried off toward Whitney and the others. Wow. She couldn't stand to be around me for five seconds.

I took a deep breath and turned to my parents. "Come on," I said, my head hanging. "Let's gorge."

• • •

After lunch, I sat on the edge of Phoebe's freshly made bed and dialed the number for Daniel's room. My knees were pressed together and my shoulders were hunched as I gripped the phone. What was I going to say? How was I going to keep him from hanging up on me?

Hey, Daniel, we need to talk . . .

Nah, too cliché.

I didn't kiss him! He kissed me!

True, but too defensive.

Why the hell are you calling Sage instead of me the night before nationals?

Yeah, that'd work.

But it didn't matter, because all the phone did was ring and ring. Finally I got the picture and hung up.

Dropping back on the bed, I stared up at the ceiling and tried to get a grip. There were too many conflicts swirling through my mind.

Like Steven, for instance. Where on earth had Steven gotten the idea that I liked him? Was I sending some kind of signal? No, not possible. The only person I sent signals to was Daniel.

And what *about* Daniel? Apparently *he* thought I liked Steven too. How clueless was he? I still couldn't believe that he hadn't given me a chance to explain. Kind of like the squad. Why wouldn't anyone let me explain myself? It was so frustrating!

Why does it seem like you have so much explaining to do lately? the little angel on my shoulder asked.

I swallowed hard, my chest growing heavy. The angel kind of had a point. Only a person who messes up a lot has to explain a lot. Right?

Suddenly the door opened and slammed and Mindy came storming into the room, all flushed.

"Do you know where I just was?" she demanded.

I sat up straight, my heart pounding. "Uh . . . no?"

"I was just in the gym with Phoebe, trying to get her to stop crying on the treadmill!"

"She's crying? What's wrong?" I asked, sliding forward.

"You're what's wrong!" Mindy said.

"Me?" *Again*? I thought.

"What exactly is your problem?" Mindy asked me, hands on hips.

"My problem? I thought we were talking about Phoebe!" I said, standing. I was a little taken aback by the level of Mindy's ire. She was usually so mild and quiet. I had never seen her like this before.

"We're talking about the fact that you've been acting totally selfish ever since we got here!" Mindy said. "What's the deal?"

"This again?" I shouted, throwing up my hands. "Okay, fine. My *problem* is that everyone wants to control me. Dye your hair, wear these clothes, don't leave our sides for a split second, don't talk to your other friends. What is this, a high school team or a military prison?"

"You are such a baby," Mindy said, looking at the ceiling.

I blinked, stung. "What?"

"Listen to yourself! You're on a squad! A competition squad! And like it or not, that means making some sacrifices. You knew that going in!" she said. "Don't you remember how serious that first meeting was?"

"Yeah, but—"

"But nothing! This is so not you!"

That seemed like a common opinion today. An opinion I was sick of hearing. "Maybe it is me! Maybe you're all just pissed off because I'm not acting like the rest of you," I said defensively.

"That's not what I mean and you know it," Mindy shot back in a tone I didn't think she was capable of. "You're being so selfish, you don't even know what's going on around you. Want to know why Phoebe was crying?"

I kind of had a feeling that I didn't.

"Did you even notice that her parents are the only ones who haven't shown up here?" Mindy asked.

My heart dropped. I hadn't, in fact, noticed that. No wonder she was acting so weird when the caravan showed up yesterday. And before, when my mom asked her to join us. I should have said something. I should have insisted that she come along. But I had thought she was mad at me like everyone else.

When has that ever stopped you from making an overture before? the shoulder angel asked me.

"She told me just now that you're the only one who knows everything about what's been going on with her family, but you haven't even checked in with her," Mindy said. "She's really upset that you've basically abandoned her, but do you see her getting all whiny and mopey and letting it affect everyone else? No! Because she doesn't want to bring the team down. You, of course, don't seem to care about that. All you seem to care about is yourself."

Omigod, I was evil. I was the most evil-est person in the entire world. Forget Tara and Sage and the crazy Black Bears captain. I *was* the devil in pleats.

Apparently Phoebe *hadn't* let Tara in on everything, the way I had hoped and assumed. She had wanted to talk to me after practice yesterday and I had completely bailed on her for Becca. And I hadn't even asked her about it since, instead focusing on the fact that she was part of the anti-Annisa attack the night before. I should have been able to put that aside. I should have remembered how upset she was. What kind of friend *was* I?

Mindy sat down on Tara's bed, looking shell-shocked. "Wow," she said. "I don't think I've ever yelled like that. Like, ever."

"Mindy, I am so . . . so . . . sorry," I said. "I just—"

"Phoebe's the one you owe an apology to," she said, taking a deep breath. It might have been the first time she had pulled in any oxygen since walking into the room. "Look, as your friend, *I* understand how much you like Daniel and *I* don't think you should have to dye your hair. I just don't think all this stuff should affect the squad. Do you even realize that we wouldn't be here at nationals if it weren't for you? You're the one who brought this team together before regionals when you came up with that plan to help Phoebe. We never would have won that day if it hadn't been for that."

Back before regionals, Phoebe had confided in me that the reason she and her mother had moved in with her aunt was because her parents were splitting up. Knowing that she hated her new room, I had rallied the squad together to sneak in and repaint and decorate it for her. Phoebe had been touched by the gesture and had completely bounced back. Sometime between then and now, however, things had clearly gotten worse.

I didn't know what to say. I wasn't even sure if I *could* speak past the lump in my throat.

"But now, thanks to you, we're all falling apart again," she said.

She pushed herself up and walked out of the room, near

tears. It was like she had spent up all her energy and now she was ready to crumble. I understood the feeling.

For a long while after she left the room, I just stood there, frozen. My question had been answered. What the squad had done to me didn't even compare to what I had done to them. This all started with the hair-dyeing thing, and it wasn't like all of them were even behind that idea. But me? Well, I had disappointed *everyone*. I didn't think I was ever going to forget the look of betrayal on Mindy's face.

After checking the gym for Phoebe, who wasn't there, I retreated to our room to wait for her. We still had a couple of hours before dinner and technically I should have been working out or running or trying to get some sun, but I wasn't in the mood. All I wanted to do just then was talk to Phoebe and sort things out. If I could sort them out with her, then maybe I could fix things with the rest of the squad as well. I had decided to take it one Fighting Crab at a time.

I didn't even realize that I had fallen asleep until there was a loud knock on my door. I sat up straight and looked around. Still alone. But that knocking sure was persistent.

Maybe it was Daniel! Or maybe Phoebe had forgotten her key! I jumped up and whipped the door open without even checking the peephole.

"Hey," Jordan said with a mischievous grin. "Want to have a little fun?"

Maria Rinaldi and Corey Frezza, another member of the Beavers, were standing just behind her. As much love as I have for my best friend, I was kind of disappointed to see her there and not one of the dozens of people I had to apologize to.

"What kind of fun are we talking about here?" I asked. For some reason, the tiny hairs on the back of my neck were standing on end. There was a definite naughty vibe in the air.

"Please. You're coming with us," Jordan said, grabbing my wrist. I just had time to check that my key card was still in the back pocket of my jeans before the door slammed closed.

"What are we doing?" I asked as we started to jog.

"We're going to have a little fun with the Black Bears," Corey replied. "They're probably thinking they got away with turning us in last night."

"Yeah, right. When it comes to Becca and Gia, no one gets away with anything," Maria said with a laugh.

"Okay, I really don't like the sound of this," I told them as Maria shoved open the door to the stairwell. I had the same exact feeling I'd had the moment I realized my squad was planning on tagging West Wind High a few weeks ago. That "we are so going down for this" feeling. And, of course, we had gone down. Big-time.

"Come on, Annisa! Live a little!" Jordan called to me, her voice echoing off the walls and down the well.

My steps slowed as I climbed the stairs behind them. I could just turn around and go back to my room right now. I had people to talk to. And this getting-back-at-the-Black-Bears thing could not be innocent. But I kept following anyway. I didn't want to disappoint Jordan. I barely ever got to see her and now I was going to bail on her?

We got to the twelfth floor and the rest of the squad was waiting by the ice machines. The already uneasy feeling in my gut intensified when I saw that Lara Lefkowitz was toting a bag full of stink bombs and marbles. Lara's little brother Lenny was, like, the stink-bomb king of the Northeast. He'd gotten tossed out of every grade school, summer camp and Hebrew class he'd ever attended. And the marbles? That had to be inspired by the time Gia's stepmother had ended up in traction after her little sister had left her marbles all over the kitchen floor. There was a rumor that Gia had actually done it—on purpose—but I had always chosen not to believe that.

"Um, you guys?" I said, my palms growing sweaty. "What are we doing exactly?"

"We're just gonna leave the Black Bears a few presents in their rooms," Corey said with a shrug as the others giggled.

"*And* steal their competition uniforms," Maria added.

A couple of the girls high-fived and I looked at Jordan. She could not be okay with this. It was cruel. It was dishonorable. It was *cheating*.

But Jordan was smiling with the rest of them.

"Come on! It's time to meet Gia and Becca," someone whispered. Together everyone slunk out of the ice machine area and started down the hall. I grabbed Jordan's arm and held her back.

"Are you kidding me with this?" I said.

Jordan rolled her eyes. "It's not that big a deal. Come on!"

Not that big a deal? Was she insane? They could get disqualified for this! Worse, they could get arrested. Wasn't this breaking and entering? And robbery? And, I don't know, reckless endangerment?

I do love my *Law & Order*.

"Jordan! Wait up!" I said, following her around the corner.

As soon as we got there, we both stopped in our tracks. The rest of the team was at the other end of the hall, but right in front of us, making out all pressed up against a door, were Bethany Goow and Chuck the Artiste.

205

"Whoa," I blurted.

They sprang apart. Bethany's dark-as-pitch lipstick was all smudged around her lips and on her chin. It had left Chuck's face looking bruised.

"Oh, hey, guys," Bethany said, super casual. "What's going on?"

Jordan and I both looked at Chuck. He got the message quickly and opened the door to his room. "Call me later," he said to Bethany.

She lifted her hand quickly, like she had already forgotten all about him. For a girl who had been freaked about alone time with the boy yesterday, she had sure moved on to nonchalant pretty quickly.

"So, what are you guys doing?" Bethany asked, looking over her shoulder at the rest of the Beavers squad. They were all gathered in a huddle at the other end of the hall now.

"Apparently, we're stink-bombing the national champions," I said wearily. "Wanna come?"

"Hells yeah!" Bethany said, lighting up. Why was I not surprised?

"You're not invited," Jordan said flatly.

"What?" Bethany and I said in unison.

"Annisa, this is something we're doing as a squad," Jordan said. "No outsiders."

My mouth dropped open. Since when did Jordan exclude anybody from anything?

"Hate to point out the obvious, sister friend," Bethany said sarcastically, "but Annisa isn't *on* your squad."

Jordan looked at me. Ouch. There was no arguing with that.

Suddenly the stairwell door opened and I jumped, feeling like the feds were going to descend upon us at any second. (Okay, maybe I watch *too* much *Law & Order*, but still.) It wasn't a bunch of dudes in blue jackets, though. It was just Becca and Gia. They were both flushed and halfway to manic.

"Annisa! You came!" Becca said, all psyched. She grabbed my wrist and started pulling me toward the others at the end of the hall. "Come on! Gia flirted with one of the bellboys until he stole us the keys to the Black Bears' rooms."

"They're all downstairs giving interviews for some local broadcast," Gia said with a snarl. "It's now or never."

"I'm gonna go with never," I said. I tore my arm out of Becca's grip and her sapphire ring made a scratch in my skin.

"What?" Jordan asked.

"Look, you guys. This isn't right," I told them, my heart palpitating. "It's not only totally mean, but it could get you kicked out of here. Is that what you want?"

Becca's face fell, but she quickly regrouped. And laughed. "I always knew you were a wuss, Gobrowski," she said.

I felt a pang in my chest, but stood my ground. "Not wuss enough to fall for that reverse-psychology crap."

From the corner of my eye I saw Jordan watching us, shifting from foot to foot. Becca stepped right up to me, her face inches from mine.

"You know, I really thought you were one of us," she said, her green eyes flashing. "But now I see I was wrong."

"You know what, Becca? I'm not one of anyone," I said, trying not to visibly shake. "I'm just me. And I want to compete tomorrow. And I don't want to go home knowing that

I cheated or that someone got hurt because of me. I guess that's the real difference between us."

Becca snorted and backed up a bit. "Maybe you *should* dye your hair," she said, shaking her head. "You've totally changed."

I didn't really see it that way. If I had been here last year with the Beavers and they had suggested sabotage, I'd like to think that I would have said no then too. But who knows? All I could be sure of was that I was saying no now. And if that meant I had changed somehow, then I had clearly changed for the better.

I took a step back, away from her and toward Bethany. As of that moment, I had lost all respect for Becca Richardson. Becca hit me with one last scoff and then turned and walked toward the squad. Gia snapped her teeth at me, psycho that she was, and followed. Jordan didn't move.

"You don't have to do this, Jor," I said, feeling pretty high after sticking up to Becca. "You know what happened to me during the whole prank-war thing. I ended up in *jail.* You guys could get in serious trouble. This isn't like you."

"Omigod, Annisa! If I hear one more story about how much you've done with your new squad or how I should learn from your cheer *wisdom*, I swear I'm going to heave!" Jordan shouted.

I blinked, totally taken aback. Jordan had never yelled at me before.

"And how would you know what is and isn't like me?" she asked, her eyes filling with tears. "You don't return my phone calls, you almost *never* call me first. You're so wrapped up in your new friends and your new life, you have no *idea* what's going on with me! Did you even know that Matt made the hockey team at school? Or that my mom got demoted? Or that I got a tattoo on my back?"

"Really?" Bethany asked. "Let's see!"

"So not the time, Bethany," I said under my breath. I squared my shoulders and looked at Jordan. Inside I was reeling from all the news that was being heaped on me, but I couldn't focus on that right now. "Jordan, how am I supposed to know any of that if you don't tell me? I mean, you didn't even tell me that you guys were competing!"

"How am I supposed to tell you any of it if you're not around to tell?" she asked.

I swallowed hard. "Well, what did you want me to do? Move to Florida and not make any friends?"

"No, but you don't have to show off all the time either! About how great they all are and how amazing your squad is and how perfect your life is," Jordan replied. "It's like you don't even miss me!"

"Of course I miss you!" I told her.

"Could've fooled me," she said.

"Jordan! Come on!" Becca whisper-yelled from the other end of the hall, growling on the "on."

"I have to go," she said. Then she turned and ran to catch up with the others.

For a moment, I couldn't move. I couldn't breathe or think. I had endured more drama in the past two days than every character on the WB last season combined.

"Wow," Bethany said finally. "The Jersey me is a little scary."

"Come on. Let's get out of here," I said.

"So, you gonna drop the dime on them?" Bethany asked as we walked to the elevators.

"No. I don't know," I said. "Let's not talk about it."

My legs were shaking. I felt like everything I knew had been blown to bits. What had happened to Jordan? And to Maria? In the past I could always count on them to be the levelheaded ones, but they were acting totally whacked now. The whole squad was. Yesterday, Becca had scolded Gia for smoking because she didn't want to get kicked out of the competition, and now they were breaking into another squad's rooms!

Revenge really meant a lot to Becca Richardson. Not a healthy way to live.

"Eh, don't worry about the Jersey girls," Bethany said as she hit the down button. "I still think you're cool. And really, what more could you want in life than my approval?"

I managed to laugh and leaned my head on her shoulder. "You might want to fix that lipstick," I said.

"And erase the evidence that I've been kissed?" she said. "Not likely."

We stepped into the elevator and started to sink. I wasn't even paying attention to where I was going. *What more could I want in life than her approval?* I knew it was a joke question, but it got me thinking. What *did* I want?

Well, I wanted to be happy again. I wanted to have fun cheering with my squad. I wanted my friends not to hate me. I wanted them to know that I was with them one hundred percent. What I wanted was my life back.

"Coffee?" Bethany said as the doors slid open to the lobby.

My pulse was racing with excitement. Suddenly I knew what I had to do. I knew where I belonged.

"I have to get back to the squad," I said, starting to smile.

She stopped the doors from closing with her arm and stared at me. "Oh, God. Do you have, like, the theme from *Gladiator* playing in your head right now?" she asked.

"Actually, it's 'Look at Me, I'm Sandra Dee,'" I said.

Bethany was clearly perplexed.

"I'll explain later," I told her.

Bethany rolled her eyes and released the doors. "Go with God," she said as they slid closed. I cracked up laughing.

• • •

By the time the elevators had reached my floor again, I had figured out exactly what I was going to say to Tara and the rest of the squad. I was practically wringing my hands with nervous energy. Then the doors opened and I forgot every last thing I had planned.

Daniel Healy was standing right in front of me.

"Oh, hey," he said.

"Yeah . . . hey," I replied.

I half expected him to get into the elevator and disappear, but he just stood there as I stepped out. Okay, now I needed a whole *new* speech. I shoved away the cheerleading file in my brain and opened the Daniel file. Unfortunately, only a taunting jack-in-the-box popped out of it.

"Listen, I'm really sorry about—"

"I wanted to say sorry for—"

We spoke at the exact same time. Then laughed.

"You go," Daniel said.

"I just wanted you to know that there is absolutely nothing going on with me and Steven," I said. "Less than nothing. We're talking negative numbers here."

Daniel smiled. "I know."

"You do?" I asked.

"Yeah. I kind of . . . talked to him today," he said, pacing backward a few steps. He pushed his hands together and flushed, looking at me with this adorably tentative face.

While it was adorable, I now had a vision of *Daniel* hanging *Steven* out of a window by his ankles. Not that he would ever do that. Although, if he had Lumberjack Bobby Goow and his brother and Carlos cheering him on . . .

"What do you mean?" I asked. "I mean, what did he say?"

"He said he kissed you and you didn't kiss him back," Daniel told me. "He said you weren't into it. So . . . *I'm* sorry. I jumped to conclusions."

"It's okay."

I couldn't have been more relieved to know that Steven knew what was what. It would make my next encounter with him far easier. Still awkward, but easier.

"It's just, I don't go out on a limb all the time," Daniel said. "When I saw you guys, I was surprised, but not *that* surprised. It was almost like I was *expecting* to get crushed."

I smiled at his honesty. "I would never crush you."

Daniel laughed. He reached out and ran his hands down my arms, then held my hands. It was so nice to be near him, I totally forgot that I was a makeup-less blob of dirty sweatshirt and jeans.

"I should have known that," he said.

Standing there with my hands in his, the bliss only lasted so long. It took mere seconds for all the doubts to come rushing back. The Sage phone calls, the fact that he had never asked me to be his girlfriend. I was so happy to be with him, but at the same time I didn't want to be thinking about all this stuff every single time we were together. Enough was enough.

"Daniel?" I said.

"Yeah?"

"How come you freaked out when I asked if you were my boyfriend?" I asked.

He sighed and looked down the hallway. "It was just so out of nowhere," he said, hazarding a glance at me. "Call me old-fashioned, but I kind of wanted to ask *you* out. I mean, you kissed me first and everything. I wanted to get to do *something.*"

A laugh exploded from me that sounded so much like a cackle, I blushed. But I couldn't help it. What a relief.

"Plus, to be honest, I thought you liked Steven," he said. "I kept seeing you guys together at school, and he walked you home. I mean, *I'm* usually the one who walks you home, and—"

I was laughing really hard now. So hard my eyes watered. And Daniel was giving me that freaked-out look.

"Sorry," I said, waving a hand. "I just . . . sorry." How could Daniel ever be jealous of anyone else when all I wanted was him? "You're just . . . too cute."

Daniel flushed. "Thanks, I think. I mean, is it good to be so cute that you make someone hysterical?"

"I'm done now," I said. "So you were never getting back together with Sage?"

"Sage? Are you kidding me?" Now it was his turn to laugh, but I wasn't finding it funny. I closed my eyes and finally just let it go.

"I saw your number on her caller ID," I said. "I know you called her the night before we left for nationals."

There was a moment of silence and I opened my eyes. "My cell number?" he asked flatly.

I felt like someone had knocked me over the head with a sledgehammer. Duh! Whenever Daniel called me, it was from his cell. I don't think he had *ever* used his home number since I had known him.

"No. Your home number," I admitted.

Daniel nodded and sort of half smiled. "Well, a lot of the guys were at my house that night. Anyone could have called her."

"Really?" I said, relief rushing through me all over again.

He nodded. "Sage has her own stuff going on. But I promise you, it has nothing to do with me."

Oooh . . . juicy. "Care to elaborate?" I asked.

"Not really. You'll have to ask her yourself," Daniel said. "But believe me, the last person I want to think about is Sage."

Ah, music to my ears.

"C'mere," he said, wrapping me up in his arms. I grinned up at him happily. "Sages are a dime a dozen," he said, touching his nose to mine. "You are one of a kind."

Oh . . . my . . . God! Could he be any more perfect?

I couldn't believe that we had put ourselves through all this drama. We had both been jealous for no reason! Why didn't we just *talk* to each other? I vowed that from then on, I would never jump to conclusions again.

Yeah, right.

"So, I have this question I've been wanting to ask you," Daniel said quietly.

"Yeah?" I asked, pulling back.

"Annisa Gobrowski, will you be my girlfriend?" he said. His face was so serious, I almost cracked up again. Almost.

"Yes! Yes, yes, yes!" I said.

He smiled and then leaned in to kiss me. Inner squeal of delight! I was kissing my very first official boyfriend! I was kissing the most perfect guy in the known universe!

This day was turning right around.

Standing outside my hotel room, I could tell the entire squad was gathered inside. The gab level was off the charts. I swallowed back a massive lump of fear and squared my shoulders. I pictured them all standing in a line by the windows like a firing squad. This was not going to be pretty.

Just do it, ya wuss, I told myself. I opened the door.

Everyone in the room fell silent. From what I could tell on first glance, all fifteen of them actually *were* present. Tara, Whitney, Felice, Lindsey and Kimberly were talking on Tara's bed. Chandra, Mindy and Jaimee were sharing a bag of popcorn over by the window. Phoebe sat on the floor between the beds, talking on the phone. Karianna and Sage were sprawled across the other bed, reading magazines. Erin was in the corner, pumping her biceps with eight-pound weights. Maureen and Michelle were watching TV on the floor. Autumn was trying to meditate.

"Mom, I'll have to call you back," Phoebe said. She reached behind her and hung up the phone.

"All right, before anyone says anything, I want you all to know I'm ready to do the right thing," I said, raising my hands. "I'm sorry for skipping dinner and for lying about it. I'm sorry if I haven't been there for you the past couple of days," I said, glancing at Phoebe. "I'm sorry if I've complained."

I took a deep breath.

"But I also know that 'I'm sorry' doesn't always cut it, so I want to prove to you guys that this squad is important to me. That I am dedicated to you guys, no matter what."

Don't do it! a little voice in my mind shouted. *Don't, Annisa! Don't!*

For once, I couldn't tell if it was the angel or the devil, but I bit back the advice and took the plunge.

"So I'm going to do it," I said, closing my eyes. I swear I almost choked on the words. "I'm going to dye my hair."

"Yes!" Tara cheered, standing up.

"No!" Mindy wailed.

"Annisa, you can't!" Autumn intoned.

"Yes, I can," I said, sticking to my guns. "If that's what you guys need me to do to prove myself, then I'm going to do it."

"You heard the girl! Let's go!" Tara said.

"But I *will* be dyeing it back first thing tomorrow," I told Tara firmly. "After we win nationals."

This cocky proclamation was met with some automatic cheers from the group. Meanwhile, my brain was hyperly listing all the things that could go wrong. What if the bleach destroyed my hair and made it frizz? What if I *couldn't* dye it back and was rendered blonde forever? What was my mom going to say? What if I looked ridiculous as a blonde and I was ridiculed and mocked and people threw stones at me?

Okay, so I have an overactive imagination. Especially in times of crisis.

"Fine," Tara said with a tight smile. "Nationals are what's important anyway."

"Tara, this is crazy," Whitney said, standing up. "Give it a rest already."

Thank you, thank you, thank you! I thought.

"No, Whitney," Tara replied, putting her arm around me. Odd. The girl had never voluntarily touched me before. "If this is what Annisa wants to do to show us how much she cares, then we should let her do it. I, personally, think it's the perfect way for her to make everything up to us."

Everyone in the room looked at everyone else. They were all gauging the situation, weighing the options. They could either stand up and defend my right to brown hair, or they could make Tara happy. Unfortunately, I could see the vote wasn't swinging my way. And it wasn't like I could blame them. I *was* volunteering. Why rock the boat when there was no reason to? We were all seasick enough after the last couple of days.

It was really going to happen. No one was going to step in and save the day. I was going to dye my hair. I had made a decision and it was time to be brave. Time to grin and bear it.

"Okay," I said, clapping my hands. "Let's do this."

• • •

Five minutes later, I was sitting in a chair in front of the sink, a towel wrapped around my shoulders. Chandra, the only person with publicly acknowledged hair-dyeing experience, had been elected to do the deed. She pulled on the clear plastic gloves and reached for the dye bottle. I gulped as she twisted the top off. As many people as possible had crammed

219

themselves into the primping area, and the rest of the squad was whispering just beyond the door. The anticipation was thick.

"Oh, that stuff stinks," Whitney said, holding her nose as the peroxide stench assaulted our nostrils.

"You put *that* on your *hair?*" Autumn said, wrinkling up her face. "That cannot be healthy."

"You gotta do what you gotta do," Chandra said with a shrug.

Sage twittered with glee.

"You sure about this?" Chandra asked me, looking doubtful.

I eyed her hair. The roots, the shagginess, the split ends. Then I stared at my reflection—at the dark hair I'd gotten from my dad. What the hell was I *doing?*

"Uh . . . yeah . . . I guess," I said.

This is not an Extreme Makeover. *It's just hair. It's just* hair! *People change their hair all the time. Look at Renée Zellweger and Xtina and Cameron Diaz and Mandy Moore and—*

But this was not a professional Hollywood color. This was a five-dollar box of chemicals from CVS. Who knew what kind of uncategorized subset of freak I was going to be when it was over?

"Well, here goes nothing," Chandra said.

Mindy and Jaimee clutched hands and closed their eyes. Whitney turned around and walked out of the primping area. I squeezed my eyes shut and waited for the smelly goop to hit my scalp. Would it burn? Would it be cold? Would it drip into my eyes and blind me for life?

Oh, God . . . Oh, God . . . Oh . . .

"Stop!"

My eyes flew open. Tara grabbed Chandra's arm and yanked it away from me. She took the bottle of dye out of her hands and dropped it on the counter. I wouldn't have been more surprised if she had just bulldozed the hotel down around us.

"What?" I asked. "What happened?"

"I can't believe you were actually going to do it," Tara said, looking flummoxed.

"*What?*"

I was so confused, I think that was the only word left in my vocabulary.

"I appreciate it, Gobrowski, but I can't let you do it," Tara said. "I can't let you destroy your hair for us."

"But this is all you've talked about for, like, a week!" I blurted.

Shut up, Annisa! Shut up!

"I know, but I changed my mind. It's too extreme," Tara said. "I mean, that stench! That can't be good for anyone. Just look what it's done to Chandra's head!"

"Hey!" Chandra protested.

"I'm sorry, honey, but the girl is right," Whitney said, rejoining us. "You have more splits than the U.S. gymnastics team."

Chandra grumbled and ripped off the plastic gloves.

"And besides, you were right the other night at Chandra's. We can't make this big of a change the night before the competition. We could totally jinx ourselves," Tara said. "What was I thinking?"

"Oh, *man*," Sage said, throwing her hands up and walking out. I guess the show was really over. I felt faint with relief.

"You really were going to do it, weren't you?" Tara said, looking at me in awe.

"Yeah, I was," I said.

Tara grinned. It was the first genuine smile I had seen on her face in days. "Well, that's good enough for us, right, girls?" she called out.

"Yeah!"

Everyone shouted and cheered and Mindy threw her arms around me, hugging me so tight, I had to hold my breath. I whipped the towel off and stood up, looking at my reflection in the mirror—at the reflection of all those happy faces around me.

It was a close call, but I was still a non-blonde. I was still me! And for the first time in days I was sure that I was right where I belonged.

• • •

That night I smiled at myself in the mirror as I brushed my teeth. As quickly as everything had fallen apart, it was put back together again. Dinner with the squad had been all kinds of fun. The Black Bears kept trying to hit us with their mind games—talking smack about us and everyone else in the room—so we just kept talking louder and louder and louder until we were so loud, we drowned them out. Finally they gave up and left before dessert.

Score one for the Fighting Crabs!

After we finished eating, I pulled Phoebe aside and we walked out to the pool to talk. She told me that her parents were officially getting divorced. It was all a big mess and they weren't speaking anymore. As a result, each had ditched the competition, concerned that they might bump into the other. I didn't have much in the way of words of wisdom for her,

222

having never been through anything like this myself, but I listened to everything she had to say and in the end, she assured me she felt better.

Especially after I promised never to ditch her in a moment of need again.

Now she was snoring in her bed, emotionally and physically exhausted. I hoped she would feel even better in the morning.

"Hey," Mindy said, joining me by the sinks. Her long hair was back in a shiny ponytail and she was wearing light blue pajamas with Oreos drawn all over them. Sweet dreams!

"Hey," I replied. A little sizzle of discomfort crackled through me. Mindy and I hadn't talked much since the hissy fit to end all hissy fits.

"I'm sorry about before, Annisa. I don't know what happened to me," she said.

"What do you mean?" I asked.

"In case you didn't notice, I went a little nuts," she said. "I don't think I've ever lost it like that before. I'm thinking it was nerves."

"You're apologizing for that?" I said. I spat out my toothpaste and rinsed my mouth. "I kind of thought I deserved it."

"You did?" Mindy said, wide-eyed. "Well, maybe you did. A little."

I laughed. "You know, maybe you should freak out more often. It's not good to keep everything all bottled up, you know? If you do, then you end up—"

"Spewing all over one of your best friends like a shaken soda bottle?" she finished with a smile.

"Exactly."

"You know, it *was* kind of cool, saying what I actually

thought for once," Mindy said, running her purple tooth-brush under the tap.

"See?"

She picked up her toothpaste and knocked over the little bottle of conditioner that had come with the hair dye. We both looked at the kit, which was still laid out on the counter, the gloves in a ball by the bottles and packaging.

"I didn't even realize that was still here," Mindy said. She placed her toothbrush and toothpaste down and reached out her hand to me. "Garbage can?"

Grinning, I picked up the little plastic garbage container and gave it to her. She held it just under the lip of the counter.

"Wanna do the honors?" she asked, raising her eyebrows.

Feeling giddy, I reached out and used the back of my arm to swipe the whole kit into the trash. Mindy tossed it back under the counter and we high-fived.

"I think I'll take this out to the Dumpster," Mindy said, yanking the bag out of the garbage can and slinging it over her shoulder. "When it comes to Tara, you can never be too careful."

"Thanks, Min," I said.

"You know, I have a feeling we're going to kick a little butt tomorrow," she told me.

I grinned in response. "I hear that."

The next morning, I came downstairs for breakfast in my blue SDH shorts and white Crabs T-shirt—just like the rest of the squad. Mindy, Autumn and I were bringing up the rear, playing Who's Hotter? (we were on Orlando Bloom vs. Ashton Kutcher), when suddenly the rest of the team stopped in its tracks.

"Oh, God," Whitney said under her breath.

"What happened?" Jaimee asked.

And suddenly, they were all looking at me.

"What?" I asked, my smile quickly fading. "What's going on?"

That's when I saw them. Two guys up on tremendous ladders, working on the "Congratulations, Finalists!" banner. They were painting big red letters over the Northwood High School Beavers. Big red letters that spelled out DISQUALI-FIED. Steven stood underneath them, snapping pictures.

"That's a little uncalled for," Whitney said.

Of course, she didn't know what had happened the night before. Suddenly all I could think about was finding Jordan. Was she okay? Had anyone gotten hurt? What had *happened*?

Steven raced over and got all up in our faces, capturing our reactions on his camera. I squeezed my eyes shut and turned away.

"Uh, now's really not the time, Schwinn," Chandra said.

He lowered the camera. "Actually, Annisa, I was kind of hoping we could talk."

Wow. So not what I want to do right now, I thought.

Luckily I was saved by the bell. The elevator behind us pinged and the doors slid open. Half the Beavers squad jostled their way out with their bags, their heads sunk so low, they looked like hunchbacks. Jordan wasn't there. My squad parted to let them through and everyone blatantly stared. Even Gia looked chagrined. I didn't think that was possible.

Everyone in the lobby grew hushed as the Beavers did their walk of shame to the front door. It couldn't have been more humiliating.

The second elevator opened and Jordan trudged out with the others, adjusting her bag strap on her shoulder and clutching her black winter jacket. Forgetting all about Steven for the moment, I fell right into step with her.

"Hey. . . . Everything all right?" I asked.

"Not exactly," she replied. She noticed the disqualified sign and averted her eyes. "We're going home, obviously."

"What happened?" I asked.

"We got caught," she replied flatly. "One of the Black Bears came back to the room for her body glitter and the rest is history."

Ugh. Snagged by a body-glitter girl. Could there be anything more tragic?

"Look, I'm sorry about . . . everything," she said. "I've been acting like a total jerk."

"No, you haven't," I said automatically.

"Yes, I have. I was up all night thinking about it," she said. "I just . . . I thought it would be like old times, hanging out with you down here. But then I saw you with all your new friends and everything and you seemed so happy. . . . I just felt like a total loser."

"You could never be a total loser," I said.

"Except for right now," she replied. We both watched as Coach Martinez walked by us, talking animatedly with a couple of the cheerleading association's officials. Jordan sighed ruefully. "I guess I just let jealousy take over."

"I know what that's about," I said, thinking of Daniel and the Sage insanity. "But you have nothing to be jealous of. You are always going to be my best friend."

"Promise?" she asked, looking a little desperate for good news.

"Promise," I replied.

"Trott! Let's go!" Martinez called out. "On the bus!"

"Oh, wait!" Jordan said, digging in her pocket. She pulled out the Derek Jeter pen and handed it over. "I won't be needing it."

"Thanks," I said, my eyes welling with tears. I felt awful for the Beavers. They had worked so hard to get here and had made the finals, and for what? I knew it was their own fault, doing what they had done, but they were still my friends. It was heartbreaking watching them go. I wished we could just turn back time to last night and I could find a way to talk them out of it.

"Love you," Jordan said, hugging me tight. "Kick some ass."

"You know it," I replied.

I stepped back and waved as she shuffled through the lobby doors. Instantly, the lobby was peppered with voices, everyone speculating over what had happened. My squad gathered around me and I waited for the onslaught of questions, my heart heavy. On top of everything else, I had no idea when I would see Jordan again. Part of me wanted to run out there and get on that bus with her.

"You okay?" Autumn asked.

"Yeah. I'll be fine," I replied.

"Of course she will," Tara said. "She's a Crab."

"Let's go get some breakfast," Whitney said, slinging her arm around my shoulders. "I'm thinking something in the dough and maple syrup oeuvre."

I smiled as they ushered me toward the restaurant, making a protective shield around me in case any of the other squads got the idea to grill the last girl seen with the Beavers. It really was nice to have my friends back.

• • •

A couple of hours later, we were all backstage in our competition uniforms, our makeup done, our hair slicked back, ready to go . . . and totally freaking out. I mean, we were straight-up hyper. Jaimee was talking a mile a minute about rules and regulations and the importance of sticking our landings. Sage and Whitney were engaged in some kind of ridiculous sibling rivalry fight that, from the snippets I could hear, had something to do with a pair of purple underwear one had stolen from the other. Erin was pacing so quickly, she was a blur. Pretty much the only person who seemed calm was Autumn, and I think she had omed herself into a trance. She was sitting cross-legged on the floor, repeating her mantra with her eyes closed, but they kept flipping up now and then, revealing the whites of her eyes.

Not pretty.

Steven was taking pictures again, but luckily he hadn't

tried to get me alone since that morning. I guess he realized that right before our finals performance was not the best time to discuss matters of the heart.

"I can't believe this is it," Phoebe said, her hands clutched together. "I can't believe we're actually competing in the finals at *nationals*."

"Not if we don't find Tara and Chandra," Coach Holmes said, joining us.

"You still haven't found them?" Erin said, her voice hitting a higher octave than I had ever heard from her.

"If Tara's in her room, she's not answering the door, and no one has seen Chandra since breakfast," Coach said.

"They can't ditch us, can they?" Jaimee asked, all red in the face. Lack of oxygen will do that to you. "They wouldn't . . . right?"

"Are you kidding? Tara lives for this," Phoebe said, reaching out to rub Jaimee's arms. "She's probably just performing some kind of superstition ritual."

"That's all well and good, but we're on in ten minutes," Coach Holmes said, checking her watch. "We can't very well go out there down two squad members."

"All right, who has their cell phones?" I asked.

A dozen hands went up.

"Okay, Phoebe, you try our room phone. Kimberly, you try Tara's cell," I said. "Mindy, you get Chandra's cell number and I'll try her room. Maureen, Erin, Jaimee, check all the bathrooms on the first floor. Maybe one of them is sick."

"Got it," Erin said.

"Karianna, check the gift shop," I said. "Maybe Chandra needed a chocolate fix."

"I'm on it," Karianna said.

I grabbed my phone out of my bag and started dialing. Coach Holmes slapped me on the back. "Nice take-charge attitude, Gobrowski," she said. "Good to have you back."

"Good to be back, Coach," I said.

Just then, there was a commotion over by the entrance and one of the squads sprang apart to let a fairly crazed-looking Tara Timothy through. Her hand was over her stomach and she was so waxy, she looked like she would melt under a match. She walked over to us slowly and dropped down on a bench. Stomach flu. Had to be. We needed an IV, stat.

"Tara! Where have you been?" Whitney asked.

"I lost my socks," she said under her breath.

"What?"

Cancel the IV. She was just loony.

"I lost my lucky socks!" she exclaimed, her eyes wide. "They're gone! Just gone! I can't go out there without my lucky socks!"

Everyone exchanged disturbed glances. "Tara, calm down," Whitney said, sitting next to her.

"No! I need those socks!" Tara said through her teeth. "Everything depends on them. I've worn them every single day since regionals. If I go out there without them, we're dead."

"Uh . . . Autumn?" I said. "Maybe you should go get some of your calming essential oils?"

"Got 'em right here," she said, pulling her bag toward her.

"I need my socks. I don't understand. Where are they?"

Autumn held up a little bottle that smelled vaguely of lilac and put it under Tara's nose. Tara slapped her hand away.

"Well, where did you leave them last?" I asked her.

"I left them right on the counter by the sink last night after I used my Dr. Scholl's spray deodorant on them," Tara said. "They were there when I went to bed. I just don't get it."

My throat went totally dry and I looked at Mindy. The *counter* by the *sink*? Let's forget about how totally gnarly it was that she would leave her jacked-up socks where we kept our toothbrushes. We could deal with that later. At the moment, we had bigger problems.

"Uh . . . Tara?" I said, trying to swallow. "Did you by any chance leave them next to the hair-dye stuff?"

Tara blinked. "I think so."

Mindy groaned and tipped her head back. Can you say *nightmare*? I knelt on the floor in front of Tara. I felt like I was kneeling in front of the executioner. *Just make it quick,* I thought. *Use a sharp blade.*

"Tara, I hate to be the one to tell you this—believe me— but your socks are gone."

"What?" she blurted. If possible, she lost even *more* color. I had to act. Fast. If only to keep my captain out of a strait-jacket.

"But wait! I have something better!" I said, my heart pounding. I pulled Jordan's Derek Jeter pen out of my bag and held it up to Tara. "See this pen? It's been a powerful good-luck charm for me and my best friend for the past *two years.* I had it with me when we won at regionals. It's never let me down. Not once," I told her, feeling like I was talking to a little kid. "So here. I want you to have it."

Tara hesitated before taking the pen from my hands gin-

231

gerly. She clutched it so hard, her knuckles turned white. "You'd really let me have this?" she asked.

"I don't need it," I said confidently. "You're my good-luck charm."

"Me?" Tara said, shocked.

"Yeah, you," I said, standing. "All you guys. We're our own good-luck charm. As far as I'm concerned, *we're* the ones who got us here, not lucky pens or socks or ribbons or anything else."

"Yeah!" a couple of the girls cheered.

"So what do you say, Tara?" I asked. "Think you can go on without your socks?"

Tara stared down at the pen in her hands, breathing heavily. For a moment I thought she was going to burst into tears and tell us all we were nuts. That she was going to forfeit. But when she looked up at me, that old spark was back in her eyes—the one she had the morning of regionals. The determined-to-win spark.

"You're right," she said finally. She stood up and slapped the pen into my palm. "We don't need this. All we need is each other."

"Yeah!"

"This team kicks butt, right?" she said, earning another cheer. "We beat everyone else at regionals. We beat the West Wind Dolphins!"

"Hell yeah!" Whitney cheered.

"And now we're going to go out there and bring this competition to its knees!"

"Yeah!" We all clapped and cheered and hugged.

"Let's do it!" Tara shouted, getting herself all riled up.

"Uh . . . there is still one small problem," Phoebe said.

"What's that?" Tara asked, grinning.

"We can't find Chandra," Phoebe replied.

Jaimee, Erin, Karianna and Maureen all raced back into the room, out of breath. "She's not in any of the bathrooms," Erin said.

"Or the gift shop," Karianna put in.

"Well, then where the hell *is* she?" Tara blurted.

"Here I am!"

We all turned around and sixteen jaws dropped in unison. Spotlights flicked on. A wind machine kicked into gear. Chandra strode into the room looking like a supermodel in cheer wear.

Her hair was brown. A beautiful, rich chestnut brown. It hung in gorgeous, creamy curls all around her shoulders. It brought out the color of her eyes and made her skin look rosy and healthy. She was a goddess.

"You look like a movie star," Autumn said, breathless.

"Is that your real color?" Sage asked, walking over to touch it.

"Close to it," Chandra said. "I made an appointment with the salon in the hotel for this morning. What do you think?" she asked, stepping over to me.

"Oh my God," I said. "It's unbelievable. But you didn't . . . I mean . . . did you do this for me?"

"Oh, please!" Chandra said, tossing back her thick mane. "I did it for me. I was sick of being a lemming. And I was even sicker of you guys constantly telling me how fried I looked. If anything, Annisa, you were just my inspiration."

"Yeah?"

"I wanted to be me again," Chandra said with a shrug. Then she grinned. "And part of the national champion cheerleading squad, of course!"

Everyone cheered and hugged Chandra, touching her beautiful locks in wonder.

"Well, I guess two brunettes are better than one," Tara said, grabbing a brush out of her bag. "Come on. Let's get you braided."

Chandra sat down on the bench and Whitney and Tara got to work brushing her hair back and braiding it so that it would be uniform with the rest of us. (Whitney and I just slicked ours back and secured it with as many bobby pins as possible.) Through all the flurry and hairspray, Chandra and I couldn't stop grinning at each other. She had taken a huge risk and she looked gorgeous. As one brunette to another, I couldn't have been more proud.

Before I knew it, we were standing on deck, waiting for the Black Bears to finish their routine. I tried not to listen to the gasps of awe or the rampant cheering coming from the crowd. Yeah, the Black Bears were good. We all knew that. But we were better.

Hey, it's good to have a little pre-competition ego on.

Finally, the Black Bears finished and ran off the mats.

"Okay, everyone! Hands in!" Tara shouted. The entire Black Bears team jostled by us, but we didn't even notice. We gathered into a tight huddle and put our hands in the center, one on top of the other. "On three," Tara said, looking around at each of us. "One! Two! Three!"

"Whaddup, Sand *Dune!*" we all shouted, throwing our hands in the air.

"And now, from Sand Dune, Florida, the Sand Dune High School Fighting Crabs!"

I cheered my lungs out as we bounded out onto the mat. The Sand Dune fans had formed themselves into a cheering section at the bottom of the stands. A huge group of families, teachers and fans in light blue and yellow shook their mini-poms and jumped to their feet. My parents and Gabe were there with Bethany and Chuck. Daniel, Christopher, Bobby and Carlos were front and center with a ton of other football players who had joined them. I couldn't have stopped grinning if I had tried.

As the music started and I bounced up into my first toss, I realized how much things had changed since yesterday's semis.

This whole cheerleading thing was fun again.

By the time I stuck my last back tuck, I knew. I knew we were giving the best performance of our lives. The crowd was getting more and more manic with every stunt, and when I was finally able to focus on my mom for five seconds, she looked like she was about to burst into tears of pride. Even Bethany and Chuck were getting into it.

I slammed into my last high V and held it, trying to catch my breath and relishing the raucous reaction in the stands. We may as well have been reality TV stars on a mall tour. I swear I thought people were going to start throwing T-shirts for us to sign.

I dismounted from the pyramid and cheered and hugged Mindy as we ran off. Backstage we were a mess of tears and high fives and laughter. It was all up to the judges now, but we all knew we couldn't have done better.

"Nice work, ladies!" Coach Holmes shouted, slapping five with Tara and Whitney. "Yeah! You nailed everything."

We whooped and cheered, feeling very pleased with ourselves. It was like walking on air, really. If I could package that feeling, I'd make some serious bling.

"Sage! Sage!" I heard someone calling in all the din.

I looked over my shoulder and saw Christopher Healy weaving his way around the other squads. Hadn't he been in the stands a minute ago? And what did he want with Sage?

"Hey! How did you get back here?" Sage shouted, bounding across to meet him.

Then, right in front of all of our gaping eyes, Christopher lifted Sage up off the ground and hit her with a seriously slobbery kiss. I swear if there hadn't been a hundred cheerleaders and coaches watching, Sage would have wrapped her legs around him.

"Omigod, *what?*" Phoebe blurted.

"Correct me if I'm wrong, but isn't that her ex-boyfriend's *brother?*" Chandra said, sticking her tongue between her teeth.

"Isn't that, like, incense?" Jaimee asked.

Felice jumped in. "Actually, it's—"

Jaimee shot her a withering look.

"Never mind!" Felice said, raising her hands in surrender.

My mind, meanwhile, was slowly putting two and two together and finally, *finally* coming up with four. This was why Daniel's home number had been on Sage's cell phone. This was why she had gotten all giggly when someone had called her from the Healys'. It wasn't Daniel on the other end of the phone, it was—gack—Christopher!

"Feeling better?" Mindy asked me, draping her arm over my shoulder as Christopher and Sage leaned into the wall, never coming up for air.

"So much," I said. Then grimaced. "But also a little disturbed."

"Ew. I can't watch this anymore," Autumn said, covering her eyes and turning away.

"My little sister, ladies and gentlemen!" Whitney announced with fake pride as Sage and Christopher nearly fell over in a lip-lock.

"Come on, you guys," Tara said, turning a few of us around. "Let's get some water."

"Um, excuse me! Barnard! What the hell do you think you're doing!?" Coach Holmes asked, looking up from her scoring breakdown for the first time.

We all laughed as we heard Sage mutter some lame apologies. My heart was as light as Marshmallow Fluff. I guess this was what Daniel had meant when he said Sage had her own stuff going on. Whatever. She could do what she wanted. All I cared about was that Daniel was really mine. Mine, all mine.

• • •

You know those cartoons where the cat sees another cat and falls in love and his heart pounds all the way out of his chest like it's on an elastic band? That's what my heart was doing while we knelt on the mat, waiting for the final announcement. I swear, it was almost painful. If Gracie Beck didn't get on with it in the next five minutes, we were going to have a couple dozen seriously premature heart attacks on our hands. I hoped the EMTs were ready.

"Why the hell did they call us out here if they weren't ready with the announcement?" Tara said through her teeth.

"The judges look completely confused," Whitney said. "Look at 'em!"

We already were. The panel of judges was passing around papers and talking in low tones, looking as nervous as a bunch of kids on finals morning. Finally the guy on the end handed a card to Gracie Beck and she scanned the list, holding her microphone in the other hand.

"Here it is . . . ," Phoebe said, causing my heart to somehow kick it up a notch.

"We don't win, we demand a recount," Tara said.

Hundreds of pairs of eyes watched Gracie make her slow ascent to center stage, walking carefully on her stiletto heels. I held my breath and clutched Mindy's hand on one side and Chandra's on the other. I was perspiring like a pig, I had to pee and I was about to need the shock paddles. God, I just wanted it to be over. I took a little comfort knowing that, win or lose, in five minutes everything would go back to normal.

"Ladies and gentlemen, as you have probably guessed, this decision was a tough one for our judges," Gracie Beck said. "I'm sure, after seeing all of the incredible performances we've had here today, you can understand why. Let's give all the squads a nice big hand for a job well done!"

I was stunned by the decibel.

"Yeah, yeah. Let's get on with it already," Tara muttered.

Whitney must have elbowed her because a second later she let out an angry "Ow!"

"We have only three prizes to give out today, but I think everyone here is a winner," Gracie continued.

More insane applause. I swear if she didn't do this soon, I was going to pee on the floor.

"So let's get to it. Our third-place squad, and winner of a $1,000 donation to their school athletic department, is . . . the Holy Cross High School Angels from Topanga, California!"

I released my friends' hands long enough to clap politely for the Angels. They went absolutely wild as they ran out and grabbed the smallest of three trophies and posed quickly with it and their check for the photographers. I wasn't sure whether to be jealous or relieved. I mean, I wanted to win *something*. And now there were only two trophies and eight squads left.

So did I hope to be called now, or did I hope not to be called so that there was still a chance at first?

Argh! This was impossible.

Mindy clutched my left hand. Chandra released me for a second, then wove her fingers through mine on the other side, clutching even tighter.

"Come on . . . come on . . . ," Whitney muttered behind me.

I wanted to ask her what she was hoping for, but there was no time.

"Our second-place squad and winners of a $2,000 donation to their school's athletic department is . . ."

Oh man, oh man, oh man!

"The Mecatur High School Black Bears from Mecatur, Louisiana!"

What? my brain shouted in surprise.

"Yes!" Tara cheered.

I was speechless. Until that very moment I didn't realize that I was fully expecting the Black Bears to win. Apparently, they were too, because it took them a second to react. The crowd went nuts, and finally the Black Bears did too. They hopped and cheered their way to the center of the mat for their trophy. They all looked fairly psyched. All except their captain. Her smile was faker than my Dooney & Bourke bag.

"You know, if they took second, there's a really good chance that we—"

"Whitney, if you finish that sentence, I swear I will never speak to you again," Tara said, her superstitious self taking over.

"Huh, tempting," Whitney said, causing all of us to laugh through our nerves.

"And now, the moment you've been waiting for—"

Obviously, Jordan's voice said in my head, cracking me up.

"Our new national champions and winners of a $5,000 donation to their school's athletic department! Give it up for—"

Anyone who says that time doesn't stop is totally lying.

"The Sand Dune High School Fighting Crabs of Sand Dune, Florida!"

I was too stunned to move, but a wave of total exhilaration pushed me up off the floor and yanked me forward. Or maybe that was just Chandra and Mindy trying to pull my arms out of my sockets. I heard myself shouting and screaming. I heard the crowd go berserk. I almost tripped racing toward the trophy with the rest of the team grabbing me and each other and shouting their fool heads off. Flashbulbs popped. Poms waved. It was all a complete and total blur.

Then I saw Tara grab the humongous trophy and hoist it over her head. We all gathered around her, lifting our hands toward the trophy and making number ones with our fingers. Steven circled us, taking pictures from every possible angle. The ESPN cameras swooped in on us, blinding us with their spotlights. As Gracie approached Tara with the microphone, I looked around at my squad mates, at Mindy, Autumn, Chandra, Jaimee, Erin, Felice, Whitney, Phoebe, Tara, Karianna, Sage—all of them—and knew that I wanted this moment to last forever.

I couldn't believe it. I, Annisa Gobrowski, was only sixteen, and my biggest dream had already come true.

Well, time never stops when you *want* it to. All too soon we found ourselves packed up and ready to go, waiting for the bus to drive around to the front door of the hotel to pick us up. The very cool thing was, we were all wearing blue T-shirts that had an SDH on the front and NATIONAL CHEERLEAD-ING CHAMPIONS! on the back. Bobby Goow and the football team had ordered them way before we had ever even left for nationals. Being Tara's boyfriend, he had really risked his life jinxing us like that.

I was really starting to like the boy.

"I wish we could just stay here," Autumn said, leaning her head on my shoulder. "I like the vibe."

"The winning vibe," Chandra said, smacking hands with Erin.

"No doubt," Erin replied.

"What're you guys gonna do when we get back?" I asked.

"We've got basketball practice on Monday," Erin said, stretching her arms above her head.

"Yeah, you guys are going to have to live without us from now on," Whitney added. "We are so gonna kick ass this season," she added matter-of-factly.

My heart sank a bit and I took a deep breath. It finally hit home that we were losing Erin, Whitney and Mindy for the winter season, which meant new tryouts for the cheer-leading squad. From what I understood, the winter season was very different. With two or more basketball games a week to cheer for, there was no competing and a lot less stress. Still, it was going to be weird bringing new people onto the team.

"I'm gonna miss you guys," I said with a little frown.

"Aw! But you'll be *cheering* for us!" Whitney said, knocking me with her elbow. "And I expect a very creative, personal cheer for every time I hit a three-pointer."

"Yeah, yeah," I said as the bus finally pulled up and hit its air brakes.

Everyone started chattering and loading their stuff under the bus. I felt someone step up behind me and turned around to find Steven standing there. For once, his camera was nowhere in sight.

"Can we talk?" he asked.

My heart thumped with foreboding. "Yeah. Sure."

We stepped off to the side and let everyone pass. This was pretty much the last conversation I wanted to have, but it would be a lot better to get it out of the way now than to be uncomfortable all the way home on the bus.

"Listen, I'm really sorry about the other night. About kissing you," Steven said, jumping right in. "I'm an idiot."

"You're not an idiot," I said.

"Yeah, actually, I am. It's just the more questions I asked about you, the more I liked you," he said, blushing. "I guess I kind of got a crush. Totally stupid."

"No, it's not," I said, trying to make him feel better. "It's sweet."

"No! It's stupid!" Steven replied adamantly. "How am I

244

supposed to be an impartial reporter if I develop crushes on all my subjects? I mean, what if I get to meet Kate Winslet one day? Apparently I'm going to be licking her feet."

I smiled. "Okay, you have a point there."

"Anyway, I'm sorry," he said. "And I'm just kind of hoping we can be friends."

"Absolutely," I told him. "Friends."

Steven smiled. "Cool."

We turned and headed back toward the bus. "So . . . Kate Winslet?"

"She's a British Botticelli goddess," Steven replied, all starry-eyed.

"Good taste," I said.

"Yo! Schwinn! Where's the camera?"

We looked up to find Bethany and Chuck walking toward us, arms slung around each other. It was crazy how totally natural they looked together after only a couple of days.

"Oh, sorry, boss," Steven said, whipping out his digital. He quickly fired off a few pics of the squad loading their bags onto the bus.

"Get a close-up of their butts," Bethany said under her breath. "Maybe we can run a 'Whose booty is it?' contest."

"Bethany!" I gasped.

"Kidding!" she replied.

"I don't get it. Why are *you* calling *her* boss?" I asked Steven. "I thought you guys hated each other."

"That was until I saw his work," Bethany said, slapping Steven on the back so hard, he tripped forward. "Boy's an ar*tiste*."

I laughed, thoroughly confused. "So, what? You're quitting the paper? Or are you just gonna be all stealth about it?"

"Nothing wrong with freelancing," Steven said with a shrug. "I gotta get my stuff out there."

"Power to the press," I said. "Or the Internet. Whatever."

"My queen? I have to leave you," Chuck said, taking both of Bethany's hands in his. He kissed one, then the other, then planted a long, deep kiss on her lips. By the time he pulled away, I think Bethany was floating somewhere over the hotel.

"Call me," she said dreamily as he lifted his hand and walked off.

"Did he just call you his queen?" I asked.

"Repeat it and die," Bethany said, still smiling.

"Duly noted," I replied.

Just then Daniel and a bunch of his friends walked out of the lobby with their bags. My heart twirled like a top when I saw him. *Mine, all mine,* my brain singsonged.

"All right, everyone! Let's load it up!" Coach Holmes called out.

Daniel walked over to me and picked up my bag. "Here. I'll get that for you. National champions should not have to lift their own bags," he said with a grin, his blond hair flopping over his eyes.

Bethany fake gagged.

"Oh, really, Your Highness?" I said, raising my eyebrows.

Bethany took the hint. "Healy! I'll meet you by the car!" she said, backing off quickly.

Daniel lifted my bag into the undercarriage of the bus, then wrapped me up in his arms and gave me a quick kiss.

"I'm gonna miss you," he said.

"It's a one-hour bus ride," I replied, smiling.

"I know," he replied. "Call me when you get home and

I'll come over. Better yet, call me when you get to the school so I can be at your house when you get there."

Terrell, who had come down with the team for the competition, made a whipping sound over Daniel's shoulder. We both laughed and parted.

"I guess I better go before more damage is done," Daniel said.

"See ya!" I replied.

I climbed onto the bus to a chorus of teasing kissy-face noises from half the football team. Little did they know, I loved every minute of it.

• • •

As the bus pulled out of the parking lot, Tara started up a chant of "S! D! H!" We all got into it, keeping the windows open and cheering as we passed by other squads and parents. Everyone cheered and waved as we went by, like we were a bus full of real celebrities. The only ones who kind of ignored us were the Black Bears. Oh, well. If they were so upset about losing, let them come back next year and try to kick our butts. That was what competition was all about.

Once we got on the highway, we all settled into our seats and Tara stood up in the center aisle. She raised her hands for quiet and slowly everyone clammed up.

"I just wanted to thank everyone for a job well done," Tara said. "Let's hear it for the national champions!"

We all whooped it up, cheering and laughing.

"But if I can get serious for a moment, I do want to acknowledge our seniors," Tara said, holding on to two seat backs as the driver hit a bump. "For some of us, this was our last competition."

"And what a way to go out!" Whitney shouted, earning another round of cheers.

"Yeah, baby!" Tara said. "But, no, seriously. Whitney, Phoebe, Felice, Lindsey, Kimberly, you guys have been the best teammates any of us could ask for. So thanks for everything. Here's to the seniors!"

"Seniors! Seniors! Seniors!" Chandra chanted, getting everyone in on the act. Phoebe and Lindsey were crying and Tara went back to hug each of them in turn, losing her balance a couple of times as the bus shifted. Steven sat on his knees, taking pictures of the emotional moment from over the back of his seat.

Once the chanting was done, a subdued silence fell over the bus. I had a lump in the back of my throat that threatened to spill over. I had tried to avoid thinking about it, but it was no longer possible. What was the squad going to be like without Tara's tyranny and Whitney's sarcasm? I couldn't even imagine not seeing them and Phoebe and the others every single day. A year from now, I wouldn't be seeing them *at all.*

Who would our new teammates be? Who would be our new captain? Would whoever it was be able to lead us back to nationals? It was impossible to believe that we could do it without the seniors.

"All right! That's enough!" Coach Holmes said, standing up. "No sad faces! This is supposed to be a celebration!"

She reached into her duffel bag and pulled out a bottle of sparkling cider, holding it out for all of us to see. Everyone *ooh*ed and *aah*ed appropriately. Then she shook it up and popped the cap, spraying us all with foam.

Through all the shrieks and shouts I saw Steven snapping

shot after shot, laughing and trying to shield his camera at the same time. Mindy and I huddled together, attempting to protect ourselves from the spray, but it was no use. Mascara ran, hair was soaked, shirts stuck to our bodies. We all looked like a bunch of drowned rats by the time it was over, but happy drowned rats. If you can picture it.

Coach took out another bottle and a bunch of blue plastic cups and poured us each a small drink. Everyone slid to the ends of their seats and lifted their cups together. I smiled, looking around at the rest of my team. We had really done it. We had come together and supported each other all the way to the title. And I hadn't even had to dye my hair. Sure, things were about to change, but for now, Phoebe was okay, Sage wasn't spouting her usual obnoxious-isms, Chandra was looking gorgeously original, and no one had mentioned the captainship all morning. For now we were all together, we were all winners, and I was just going to enjoy the moment.

"I'd like to make a toast," Coach Holmes said. "To the champions!"

Everyone grinned giddily. "To the champions!"